LUCIFER'S DAUGHTER

TRANSLATED BY TERRY ULICK

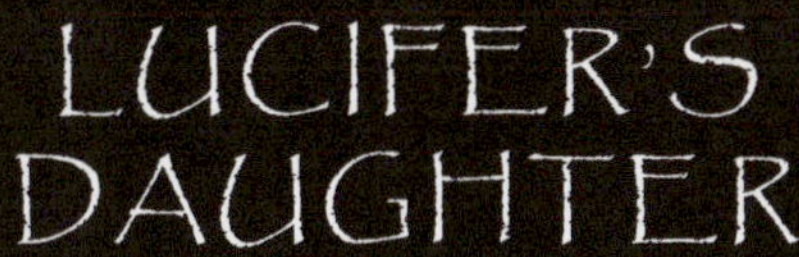

Lucifer's Daughter, Translated by Terry Ulick

Ethereal Edition

ISBN: 9798989242511

Copyright 2023, Library of Congress by Terry Ulick

Book designed, written and presented by Terry Ulick.
Book Edited by Bethany Drier

Photographs and Images Created by Terry Ulick, Copyright 2023, Terry Ulick.

Published by:

Wherever Books LLC
A Division of Renegade Company LLC
Littleton, CO 80127
www.whereverbooks.com

Roku Channel:
Wherever Books

To Bethany

Trigger Warning

If you are sensitive to obscene language, graphic descriptions of explicit sex acts, use of language describing bodies that is not anatomical and is degrading, dirty dialogue between despicable and disgusting characters, please do not read any further. This book will upset you and you will be offended.

If you are suffering from any form of physical, mental, verbal, or sexual abuse, or suffer PTSD from such abuse or other types of violence or harm, please, shut this book. It will trigger you throughout.

If you have religious beliefs based on the teachings in the Bible, either one or both Testaments, this book contains concepts and references to religion, clergy, and Christian teachings that will upset and offend you. This is not a book about the *Bible* or of religious teachings and creates its own narrative of God, Angels, and demons. It will upset you and offend you. It is suggested you stop reading now.

Know This

I, Elsa, am not Angel or human. I was created by the Fallen Angel, Lucifer. As he is my father, I am his daughter.

Made to be lust, craving, passion and all things desired by humans I began my existence knowing only what my father taught me. Using me to entice fools, he made me such where any sight of me meant instant death to anyone seeing me. To keep ones not deserving such fate safe, I kept my form and face hidden except to those who sought to take me as theirs.

Forbidden to love or be loved by any but my father I have long been alone with much time to consider the nature of lust, sin, and what I had not. Love.

In my lonely hours I scribbled the scrolls collected in this gathering. I tell of how my father, hasataan, ruined existence for all and how insane he is. I am the one made to be the next hasataan and know things no others have been witness to.

Be warned that if you follow the ways of my father, you are doomed. He cares nothing of you.

As I sit at a table made of wood from the Tree of Life once in the Garden, I have untied the sheath holding my secret scrolls to share with all who do not wish to dwell in abaddon for eternity. It is a place that has no fire, no light, no purpose and the suffering there is being in a place where there is nothing. No one wants nothing, but that is what awaits ones destined there.

Lucifer's Daughter

None choose who their
parents are. Know I did
not have a mother and
did not choose my
father.

I would be as insane
as him if I did.

Elsa

Folio I

Starting at the Bottom

Know that having no shame of body, I was naked having sex with Michael the Archangel the first time I met the Creator. I noticed He gave pause when he looked at my bottom for it is one to marvel at, and He has marveled at it all times since. I cannot say it was a look of lust or desire, sadly, for He is worthy of such a delight. No, I know such gaze, and it was not that. It was of longing. I am the only soul He did not create in all of existence, and I speak true it has since been revealed that His look held longing. He confided to Michael much later He wished he had created such perfection.

Meeting since, knowing such, after a warm embrace and staring into each other's eyes, I turn round for him to have a look, but not in such manner to be obvious to any around us. Such is not to allure or entice Him, nor is it to shame Him for not creating me. He spoke true to me one time that it was a reminder of how the nature of being omnipotent was naught but a misnomer. A myth for philosophers to ponder. I feel closest to Him when such is revealed.

Meeting each other, each time He would look and offer compliments sincere. He gazed and would ponder the mystery of what I offered. Each time He would say something only I understood while others shook their heads thinking only we had an ongoing debate. I treasure each one and have favorites when I have Vision of Him saying them to me.

"It is not that I couldn't make such wonder. It is that I didn't."

"Elsa, you are the flaw not flaw in My design. The missing thread in the tapestry of Creation."

"The only star in existence I had not considered."

"The missing chord I have longed to hear."

Thinking Him a bit hard on Himself, I could not argue the matter for He knew it true, and so did I. I sought understanding if my existence saddened Him and asked Him such.

"It is wonderful that you care for My feelings. I reveal something no other has known, and your first thought is to console Me. Thank you, Elsa. I knew you would understand that what is seen often is not what is. No, little one, I am not saddened. I am humbled. Now I can look out at Creation and wonder if there is something else having existence not Mine. You are proof that My work is not all there is. There will always be more."

Seeing no worry or sadness, I have a different way of Knowing as it is true I am not of His design or thinking. He has told me often it is a delight to talk with one who does not have His nature or way of thinking. That I am not of the same mind as all others, and that is true. My reaction to His true Revelation was something not even He had thought of.

"Father not father, I see a hope that just as Michael found me, there may be one not of Your making out there. A love that exists only for You?"

We could only look at each other and nod. I, made to be desire, was the only being that could know the answer. Or, at least see the reason for it. He had made all things except a love for Himself. He was alone.

It is true that in form I am quite small. It was my sick father's insight into the nature of form that to be the most desired of any, that I must have form that provoked a vulnerability. A need for protection. For most who are corrupt, small is to dominate by physical power. Small is thought to be weak. Fragile. Easily taken as it can offer no fight. It is a truth. The large have an advantage over the small. They are the ones who lift, not the ones lifted. I see no right or wrong in such plan. My form was to defile such purpose, and it has done so. To be large is to be mighty for the children of Earth. Males tower over females and do so often not to build or provide what ones large and mighty can offer. Instead, they use such might to take the small and feel God-like. My father not Father was knowing. He learned the day he became hasataan that once he became larger than all others, he had power over them. Since, all have cowered in fright at his sick guise. Knowing that as no other could, when he made me, he reached a new height of Knowing. Instead of a huge form to take others with fear, he made me very small. He made the next hasataan, me, to be one none would fear. I was given power over others with being all they desired, not with any might.

His insight into the nature of all Creation is what amazes the Father. He looks at me and knows I am not only the one He did not Create. I am the one who uses no might, and that is not the nature of Creation. The big fish eats the little fish, who ate the tiny things filling waters, who ate things so small they had no power to stop from being taken. To the Creator, I am the thought not Thought. He has not created any like me. I can stop the mightiest of form with but a look, a slight tilt of my head. With my lips opening slightly. My power was never to use power of form. It was to use desire to have what was longed for, what was craved but could not be had.

I offered the power of doing wrong, not right.

That has a very strong appeal to all, including Michael, my love. He has never had to say it, but he knows it is true. When first seeing me, I was a little thing reaching up for an apple but too small to reach it. Even knowing I was the daughter of the hasataan, spawn of the only true evil, he did not repel me. He came to reach for an apple to give me for I was a little thing he felt compelled to help. To show his might. To be attractive to a form he was attracted to. It made him feel his power. I made him feel he was needed.

Know that I was instantly attracted to him for that very reason. The highest and most powerful Angel could surrender to his true nature and offer his might to one who had none. He saw that he had something needed only he could give. He saw I had something no other could offer. Not holding to the nature of things, he saw the truth of things. The truth is we all have something to offer. A gift another has not. In my smile he found what he needed. Love. You will learn why my love was the greatest gift possible for I was created with the life and spirit taken from his love, Ethereal, who my sick father consumed. He ate her existence, and it flowed from him to me.

When Lucifer created me, he did so with the life of Ethereal. Her being became part of him, and it is part of me. My father knew that. In making me, it was his plan to use that to make me desired by Michael. My father did things no other could ever think of, and I am such stuff. With that, know that as with all things made, he was eternally flawed.

In making me to be the only one who could sway Michael with desire he could not deny, he did not consider that I would desire the same of Michael. To love him, not hurt him. To protect him with the might I had. I am small in form, but the most powerful in love. Love is beyond size or power. It is mightier than any form. It was unexpected. Desire to be loved humbles the most powerful being of form or spirit. It is the power that drives all things.

That is why I knew the Creator would stare at my bottom. It arouses passion in Him. He longs for one He has no power over. Only then will He know true love. It is not me, for in truth I am the daughter of his wayward son, Lucifer. We are related that way. I know He longs for one He did not create. One who He has no might over. Love is not power or control. It must be true, it must be given.

He thought such a being was not possible for He had made all things. That was once true, but then there was me. The impossible. With me, He realized the impossible was possible. I proved there could be a true love and mate for Him. Like me, but not me. When I came into being He realized there could be another not of His design or making. In me is the possibility of one He could love. Philosophers have said all things being possible, it is likely to happen. I happened, so that gives credence to such thought. Most of all I give hope to the Creator.

That is why I am desire.

I am what is not possible, probable, or follows the nature of things. I am what is wanted.

What can not be had except for the one worthy of such gift.

And, as we are friends and I am not able to say anything not true, we understand I know what no other knows of Him. When first He looked at my bottom in awe, I knew why. I kindly tease him about it as it is a thing we share. I asked him why He looks at my bottom and smiles. He looked at me with a smile that I shall forever hold dear, and told me in His quest for a love, as with all things, to reach great heights you start at the bottom.

What Else a Daughter Is

Know I have travelled every land where children, those born of Earth, dwell and roam. I have learned much of what Lucifer has done to the most innocent and the most evil. It is a sad thing to know, and even sadder for me to tell of.

At first all humans seemed without purpose, having no direction or home. It is true I have been on Earth long before cities and rulers when people roamed the land looking for food and shelter. Then as their number grew, they stayed in one land and built dwellings and worshiped sticks or clouds passing by as gods. In time some grew bold and became rulers and dictated what gods to worship or pretended to be gods themselves. People followed, looking for a land beyond the sad life they led. No ruler had an answer, and even in temples or adorned with jewels and gold they remained wanderers looking for something, anything. None were strong; all were afraid. Know that all people are the same as that has never changed.

From my first visit I saw this sad place was ever about making more sad people wandering the desert that is life here. Those who knew of the Father sought only to make more people to worship God. I was there when some fool who wished for my body said to a large gathering that he had been visited by God, commanded all should fuck and make ever more worshipers to honor Him. Looking at the tribe of people gathered, I knew there was no wish to worship a true God. They heard only that the true God wanted them to fuck endlessly and that was what they worshiped.

Fucking.

Soon the world was divided into ones who fucked to make more fools, and ones who were in service to my father, Lucifer, the hasataan. He was the one who appeared and told the one who preached to please God by fucking. To ruin all the true Father had created on Earth, hasataan needed ever more souls to feed on to be strong. He alone turned worship of God to worship of body and perversion as no human can sustain fucking without ever more perverse excitement to be aroused. All around me changed to pleasing their god by doing hasataan's wish of reducing themselves to putting fucking above all things, including God. I have no good to say of my sick father but as I am incapable of saying anything other than truth, he is good at being bad. He is clever and a deceiver.

With humans convinced that God wanted them to fuck and fuck and fuck, my father knew his hunger for taking souls would be satisfied, and the true Father would know the pain of being nothing more than a myth. He taught fools how to become rulers, how to kill and control, and offered them meaningless rewards to do his service. The history of mankind is the history of fools selling their souls for a trinket or some imagined power. That was always so, and still is. None today have any power. The power is all deception to feed the hasataan, nothing more.

Lucifer, as I shall call him hence, soon learned that humans had trouble having humans to fuck. The ones who did his bidding soon grew tired of endless slave girls or whores, and unable to get hard or fuck easy takes, were not an inspiration to their followers to make ever more souls for Lucifer to take. He tried many ways. He had such men want to fuck men or goats or children. He gave them potions to get them hard. He kept them young and strong, but they all grew tired of endless fucking no matter what it was they fucked.

Being relentless in his desire to hurt the Father, he gave such task to me. I was what else he could devise to corrupt humans. My creation is a story that none can begin to even imagine, but I continue to tell it as what it was. I will tell of it here as it explains why I ended up being Elsa, his next, his perfect sin, his daughter.

Wanting to show the Father that he too could create a being, he used his Will to do what the Creator had done. He went to the madness of his mind and there he sat, in nothingness like the Father had done before there was existence. I say again that my father, Lucifer, is relentless and has the wisdom of being a First Angel. He exists in existence — the place Father thought of long ago and has all things known, and he also exists in the nothingness of his mind. His true home is his madness. It is a place where nothing exists that any can understand for that is what madness is. There, he has nothing other than madness, and like the nothingness that was before anything existed, he is the only thing there. He is a thought, an idea, and a perversion of his own thought and idea. It was there that he thought of something worse than nothingness.

He created a nothingness that was not black or empty. His thought made nothing into pain to exist in. Even before Earth and its harsh places, his nothingness filled with grains we know to be sand. The sand is endless and like eternity it is forever in every direction. I can best explain it as if one were to float in the nothingness of the universe forever. The universe you know is empty except for a small number of stars and planets that were notions and fanciful ideas of the Father long ago. In Lucifer's nothingness, you would travel through an eternity of sand blowing relentlessly in swirls and storms that would pierce your soul like an arrow would pierce a body on Earth. The sand is madness. The universe made by God is peace.

In the sand of his mind, he has his own abaddon. Lucifer knows it is a place none can exist in, as none could ever understand the pain there. There, he is safe and free from God, his Father. In his abaddon he thought of me. What the next hasataan would be. He knew he was no longer welcome in Heaven, his only home, and sought ever to harm the Father by defiling his children of Earth. Where he aroused only fear, his wish was to create one who would arouse desire in them. One to excite them to such orgasm they would die from it. The promise of service to Lucifer was a fair exchange to have the ultimate sexual climax. A vision of me.

Knowing what all humans craved, he thought of me being the

meaning of lust, allure, temptation, attraction, desire, craving, orgasm, fucking, sucking, and a beauty far beyond any made even by the Father. I was to be the one none could deny. None could resist me, yet none could survive even a glimpse of me. Just a look from me, a hint of my attention and they would erupt into spasms of sexual frenzy and die as they came, begging only for a glimpse of me. None were ever given such honor. I was not a prize to be had. I was orgasm, the only meaning of life and the end of life for those my father chose.

With that thought, he went to the abaddon he made for fallen Angels and most all humans and there he devised a way to take all sex and passion of humans to use as seed for my making. He sent Scorpio, his first harvester of human women, on a mission to find a thousand of Earth's most beautiful virgin girls, all unspoiled by any. They were cast to his chamber below the black granite of what humans call hell. There, he had a thousand beautiful virgins once devoted only to the true God, the Creator, the Father. With his Will controlling them, he lined them in two rows of 500, all naked, all blonde, all begging him to fuck them for they craved only his serpent. For days they wailed and cried out to be fucked by the serpent as he watched.

The serpent is not a thing I have told of yet in this scroll, but I will in tomes ahead. Only know it is not something you will want to know of. The serpent is the eater of souls, the impaler of any it wishes. It comes when Lucifer is enraged or aroused. There is no way to understand how powerful and large it is. From where his cock is as Angel, the serpent appears, and it is a snake that if wished could circle the Earth or be a size to enter a hole of a woman of Earth. It becomes what it needs to be, and it is unstoppable to any except an Angel with a Blade of Will to stop it.

On the day of the virgins, the serpent grew long enough to suspend between the two rows of 500. As it grew, it snaked past each one, rubbing their nubile bodies with its head and licking their clits with its forked tongue. As it reached the last ones, they were all licking it, kissing it, praying to it, getting on it and rubbing their clits on its scales while screaming the frenzy of their first orgasms. Lucifer watched his Father's most innocent children giving adoration to his serpent, and it was then that the serpent, not seen as it was covered completely in white skin and blonde hair wrapped around it, erupted in an orgasm that shot his vile cum through all eternity and it entered his madness of swirling sand, his own abaddon. There, the wet cum full of his seed soaked much of the sand, and it formed a place forever soaked in his cum. It was a wet patch of sand in his madness. The only place that was still.

From that patch of his cum, I rose. Fully formed, fully the same as I am now, in the sand of his madness I took form, being, and was the first one made not of the Father, but of Lucifer.

All I knew when made was what I was shown when he created me. Lucifer, the serpent, and the lust of the thousand virgins craving serpent. All I knew when made was that like the virgins, I wanted only to fuck the serpent. Nothing else, for I was what was else.

There, alone for a thousand Earth years, I knelt on the wet patch of sand, waiting for Lucifer to come and fuck me. That is all I knew, and the only thing I thought of. I had no idea what I was, or how I came to be. I had no idea what I looked like, or what humans or Angels were. I knew nothing other than I wanted to fuck Lucifer's serpent and put the thousand virgins to shame as none could fuck it as well as the daughter of the serpent could. Not knowing time or boredom, I waited.

Letting me wait a thousand years to think only of fucking him, a time came when my father appeared out of the swirling storm of sand around me. At first only a strange swirl gathering in the distance, it moved closer to me, and a form took shape, and I knew it was my father. I knew nothing else a daughter could know. My father was coming for me, and I was ready to take him inside of me. I know not what else a daughter did, so thought only of that.

For the first time since created, I stood, arms out to take his serpent to me. Stopping a short way from me, he looked at me and was pleased, saying I was more beautiful than he thought possible, and then asked me if I knew what I was.

"I am what else there is for your serpent."

Then, he asked why I was created.

"To be yours to fuck."

Smiling, he asked what was my only purpose.

"To love you."

Again, he smiled slightly, looking pleased with me. His robe blew open, and I saw him for the first time without sand blowing between us. He was beautiful in every manner that I now understand. He was a first Angel, though fallen and denied the Grace of the Father. He was perfect in form, had deep blue eyes, long black hair that blew in the wind, high cheekbones, and perfect in every way. To see him was a wonder as he had the beauty only an Angel could have, although that was one of the few times he revealed it.

As his sheath, a simple tunic open in front, blew from him, I stared at his cock, knowing it was the serpent I craved. I knelt as I wanted to take it in my mouth to please him. As I knelt, I tilted my head back, opened my mouth with my tongue out fully, my eyes closed to focus only on his serpent. As he approached me, I was beyond elation or happiness for at long last I would fuck my father and please him. I could not see that he reached in the air and caught a handful of sand, and instead of serpent in my mouth, he filled it with sand.

Being made to be as him, a hasataan, my reaction was not a thought. It was a rage. Spitting out the sand I lunged at him to bite the serpent from him. All I knew was to bite it off.

With but a look, I was thrown back far enough to see him as he laughed at me. Unable to rise or move, I laid there thinking only that I needed to castrate him. He slowly walked to me, and still frozen there he told me that fucking him was all I would ever want or need, but would never have.

It was then I had my first feeling. It was not rage or anger. It was heartbreak. I wanted his love, nothing more. Not even the serpent. I wanted to love him. He stood, nodding. He was pleased and told me so.

"Daughter, you are truly as am I. You want love and nothing else. You want to give love, and nothing else a daughter can offer her father. Ah, that is what your name shall be. Elsa. Perfect. Rise, Elsa. Stand before the one you love."

I rose up and floated above the sand below me without his power or help to see into his eyes. I was shaking with the need for his affection, a desire to hold him and offer my love to him. All grew quiet in the storm of sand, and all there was at that moment was him and me. He looked sad, which saddened me at that moment. I will never forget the way his sadness felt, or how I felt once he told me of his sadness.

"Daughter, you are new, but inside you there is Knowing. I put it there. Look at me and see what not having love is. I made you to be what else there can be of me. All I know is inside of you, all my power is yours. You are hasataan as am I. When I threw sand in your mouth, and you were in a rage, what was your wish?"

I smiled for the first time.

"To bite your cock off. To destroy you."

He nodded the sad smile.

"Ah, you are hasataan. It was the perfect response to such treatment. I too felt that way long ago. I wished for something

I loved, but instead of such a love, I was denied the same as you were denied my serpent and given nothing but the pain of this sand. To be as me, you must know the pain of not being loved, or able to love any other than the one you desire. Who do you desire, Elsa?"

I only knew him, and he was the only one I could want love from, or to love. I answered the truth.

"You, father."

He paused for a long moment and I was filled with his pain. When I could stand no more, I fell to the sand, and he knelt down next to me and whispered in my ear.

"I will never love you. I will never want your love."

My whole being went into terror, feeling alone for the first time. It was horrific to feel that alone. To be in an existence where there was only one other yet filled with such love and need for love. The only one I knew said he did not love me and wanted not my love. That was endlessly worse than being alone. I had been filled with hope of him appearing one day to love me, and he spoke true that would never be. He watched and knew what I was feeling. Putting his hand over me, again I was frozen still. His look was now torment and pain beyond even mine.

"I once had the love of my Father. I know what love is to have, and I no longer have it. Each day I am lost in this sand for I am denied all love. To be mine, to be my daughter, you now know what I know. You are unloved and alone. The love you have can only be for me. Always."

Not having known tears, I knew the power he had given to me as the next hasataan. His words sliced away my reason and I thought to end him and let there be only one hasataan. Me. I will say only that I was ready to rid existence of him then, and can only wish I had been able to. I had power such, but it worked on all but him. He knew I would wish to cast him to nothingness. It was what he felt when he fell from Grace. As I summoned the demon power he gave, he smiled, then shrugged. I did not yet understand the power of a shrug from one to another. It is a way to say that what I wished for would not be, and that is the way it goes. Trying, he told me to stop for he knew my first wish was to be the hasataan. He was not so foolish as to allow that of me. He then told me of something worse. Of my need for love. At that moment, he said he had a gift for me, and it is of such importance I will speak of it later. It was a way to assure that he remained the power over me.

"If once away from this place you meet one you love, if you give them that love, I will stop it. No, you are my daughter and I would not ever harm you. I will destroy the one you love. They will suffer and cease to exist. From this day, any who want you… crave you… who even want to look at you will cease to be. That is what being of me must be. No love of your father. No one to give your love to, as I want to give love and I can not give it. Worse, it has never been wanted."

I could only look at him. It was true and it was what I was made to be. There is no word known for such a fate. Only Lucifer and I know what that is.

He took my hand and pulled me up to stand. He saw the look on my face, and he turned away, looking up. He was looking to his Father but knew He could not see. He turned back to me.

"Know that none of this pleases me. It hurts as I know your hurt. I suffer it as you do. You are my else, and now you will do my work. The hurt you feel is the hurt given to me by my Father. You will join me in making Him feel this pain. Go with the love inside you and know you will never have or give love. That is how you show your love to me. Take the love of my Father away from those who have it."

With that, he turned to sand, and I watched him join the swirls of madness around me. Then I too became sand and then took form once more, but not in his abaddon. I was in a desert that looked much the same, but it was on Earth where there were endless humans wanting love not love. Only to fuck or be fucked. As I walked, I saw a man wandering my way. As he looked at me, he died instantly as semen shot out from his sheath. I had no understanding yet of why. As I walked, I came upon a caravan of men, all leading animals with packs of goods. They had stopped and were fucking each other in their ass as they had brought no others to fuck. Approaching, I was naked, and as soon as they were able to have sight of me, they too fell dead to the sand. Each lay with their cocks standing up, squirting white streams even though they had just died.

Lucifer said any who even wished to look at me would cease to exist. By looking at me, they perished in a moment of orgasm from seeing me. I knew what he knew, and knew what caused their deaths.

Seeing me.

Though of my father, I learned that day I was not like him at all. I had no wish for them to perish in such a manner. Not fully knowing as I was new to all things, it was not the value I have of existence now. On that day I knew only it would please my father, Lucifer.

Going to the animals, camels, I rummaged through the packs they carried. The goods were many things, but I sought only one. I soon found clothing and began searching for what was needed. I followed my Knowing and found a black sheath. A burka, and it covered my entire form where no part of my body could be seen. Looking at the men, their heads and faces had been covered to protect them from the blowing sand. I found a hijab that covered my head and face, with only a small slit for my eyes to see ahead. I put it on, and knew if any approached I would close my eyes until they passed. That would be the only way they would survive being near me.

I stood there, filling myself with the words of humans. I knew what I was. To all who encountered me I was lust, desire, passion, sex, craving, longing, wanting, orgasm, erection, beauty, and death. I was the ultimate harvester of souls, taking them from the One who gave them life to hurt Him.

I was *She Who Must Never Be Seen.* For a time. Soon, my father commanded me to let ones he chose have a sight of me. Not the ones begging or poor, lost or alone. He used his power to transport me to temples or mosques, palaces or chambers of powerful warriors. I would never know when or why. I would be alone in a small house where I lived, then without notice be in front of a king, my hijab falling off my face and I would watch him be no different than the merchants who first saw me in the desert. The mighty king would open his mouth to call out, and his cock would burst from his garb and shoot his cum as he dropped dead before me, his last gasp asking what my name was.

I would see his spirit rise as a specter sent by Lucifer appeared and sucked his soul into its mouth then vanished to give it to my father in abaddon. The body before me became something I knew well. Sand, and it blew away. I knew where it went. To the abaddon that is Lucifer's mind.

The sand of his mind, the place I was made… the sand there is made entirely from the souls of all the ones he took to deny his Father their love.

Scroll III

Keep Us Together

Know I seek no forgiveness for the evil I once was for we only know that from where we came.

I knew the mind of Lucifer, and that is nothing like the mind of any on Earth or any Angel. To be Knowing, I turned within myself and wandered through mazes of sand that never led anywhere I wished to go. Sand, being fluid in nature, is ever changing and a path once taken often offered no return. Never crying out for his help when lost, in time I learned most of his knowledge. With that, I learned to navigate the sand of his madness. Looking endless and impossible at first, it was not that in any way. It was so simple I was certain that all that was obvious was anything other than deception. It is like the path he makes for the children of Earth. A straight road to abaddon. The maze was only him pondering what harm to do next, nothing more. His mind is much like a child's. He thinks only of himself and seeks simple answers.

The problem with his maze is he thinks of too many things, and that was why it seemed complex to me. Every path was a vile thought. I first considered them to be wisdom, but they were nothing such. The vile thoughts ended at a wall I thought of as indecision. It was in a place no wall was needed. He knew what was on the other side but would walk away. Soon I learned to think as he would, taking paths I knew he would. The paths with walls were distractions, nothing more. As I went the way he would, take the path he would follow, those paths led to one place.

Hurt.

Walls in the maze became certain in my mind, as it knew his. Any path taken, if it led to a place where he faced the hurt of being unloved and cast from Heaven or reminded in the smallest manner of such, there would be a wall of sand. It kept him from going there to face the truth of his decisions, all of which hurt him and in turn hurt me. It is true I wished to learn what made my father think as he did and be the one who changed all existence from light to darkness. Since I was of him, from him, I wished to not be like him and it is natural to learn what it is that you wish not to be. Such things become part of you and you don't wish to end up walking in the same direction.

Standing in the middle of a maze with so many paths leading to hurts, I stopped and questioned why I was in the maze at all. Lucifer, if he wished to keep anything from me, would not put such where I could find it. Then I thought that knowing such, it may be the very place he would hide something. A place so easily seen I would not even look there. In a search of one who could travel through infinite time and space, there are many places where a thing may be hidden. Then, a thing hidden such would be hard to reach, and even its location could be forgotten. With that I began looking in the most likely places for ordinary things to be hiding what I sought. A table near a chair. A chest holding clothes. A cup full of odds and ends. I started at the place he was most comfortable and allowed none, save me, from entering.

His mind.

Minds are filled with secrets. They are host to unwanted thoughts and memories. They are each different yet all the same. I have a sense of things given to be the temptress that I am. It was telling me the thing I wished to find was kept in my father's mind. His storm of sand which would hide anything put there.

I have told of the events of my creation, and told there was one thing I held to speak of by itself. I will complete the story now, as it is even more important than my making.

The day in his abaddon where I first met my father, after looking at me when I lunged at him, he told me he understood my action

and admired it, saying he was proud of me. He said for such
a child he had a most wonderful gift. As I watched him, still
scathing with anger, in his hand appeared something I thought
was beautiful for I had seen nothing but sand until that day. It
was a cord of crafted in fine detail. It was the symbol of what I
had wanted from him. A serpent. At one end the cord was a
serpent head, the other end a tail. I stared at it as it was a thing
unique. He told me to lift my hair, and he leaned and put the
serpent cord around my throat. It was long and he wrapped it
around my throat. Holding the head and tail, one in each hand, as
the cord fit perfectly when wrapped around me, the two ends met.
The head came alive and it bit its own tail. The head was the clasp
that held the cord tight.

Rubbing it with my hands, I felt special. I asked him what it was.

"It is me. I will always be around you and with you. It is a
necklace, a thing of wonder to have and wear. There is no other
like it."

He looked at me and told me to remember what he said. He
would always have his hands round my throat and would use
them if he thought it must be done. Then he did something most
strange. He asked if I had enjoyed my mouth full of sand. I told
him he had provoked me and like all he told me, it all hurt and
I thought him to be only a wayward Angel who felt sorry for
himself. I told him he was no father and had no reason to treat me
such. He stood, looking ashamed and appeared to be thinking of
what he had done. He looked at me and he seemed to regret his
actions. He offered a way to ease my mind.

"To do my work, I do not wish you to be thinking of the matter. I
have learned that it is fair to offer you a chance to show me I was
cruel for no reason, for you are right. There was no reason other
than to show you I have power to keep you in your place. That
you may never seek to usurp me. But with you, I will do what I
have done for no other. I will turn my back and prove to you that

it is best to get such a hurt out of your mind. I will stand here, and daughter, this one time you may take out your anger as you wished in your rage. I will not attack you. You are free to attack me."

It was true the rage was still in me, and though I had lost the need to bite his cock off, I found myself wanting to destroy him. It would be my only chance. With no caution I jumped to land on his back and claw at his Angel face from behind. He was close to me, and the distance needed only slight effort to reach him. I flew up, and just before my hands were about to grab his neck, I learned of his gift to me.

The serpent necklace tightened around my neck in an instant, came alive and pulled me with great force to the ground as it hissed at me. I tried to sit up, but it held me down with force, growing tighter with each move I made to free myself from it. I pulled at the head and tail to tear it free from me. It only grew tighter. I pulled at it from the sides, and it trapped my fingers under the cord and I could not get my hands free. Every attempt to move it or pull it away made it tighter. Looking up, I saw my father standing over me. He was not smiling or laughing for his expression was somber and I stopped struggling with the serpent chain. I couldn't speak or cry out, but he knew I tried to.

"Having powers equal to mine, I think it best to reign them in. If I need, I will pull if you hold on to any but me."

Since that moment, I have had the serpent collar around my neck to know no freedom. Having beauty, power, life eternal… all are nothing for I am not free to use them as I choose.

First Take

Know once learning to cover myself I could wander the strange land of humans. My father put no demands on me when first I came to the place made by the Creator. It was all new. Understanding visage of me meant death to humans, I covered myself and only then did I consider what was all around me.

Knowing only my father as beautiful Angel in form, I had Knowing that there was a place called Earth and the children there were humans made in the image of the Creator. Knowing is a strange quality for I knew what they were but only had understanding they looked close in form to my father. They had arms and legs, a head, and they talked. They lived in sand, had no mastery over it, and sand was not thought or mind but a lifeless thing made of form that would not change. As I walked it did not part or make way for me. It blew at me as if I were a human being. Learning that it had no will of its own, I used my Will to never allow it to touch me. My form was also my spirit and could be solid or illusion. When solid I could feel the wind and the sand, and I soon wished to be solid and feel the strange place.

My first Knowing was to do my father's bidding. I would be as a human. I would eat, drink, walk with legs, sleep, wake to do such things with each passing of day and night as the Earth circled the ball of fire called Sun. I felt the heat of the Sun and the cool of the night and I saw the stars in the sky above. I smelled food being made, heard sounds all new to me, and saw that each human was different from the other. They did not please me as they were not beautiful in spirit or form. Most seemed without the simplest Knowing.

Know the desert was the beginning of humans gathering to live and stay in one place. I found that they had a way to live together that was seldom from desire. Know they lived together for strength

as they were afraid to be alone. On my first day in a town I thought how foolish such notion was. If my father were to rise and wish them destroyed the gathering of many would mean little. He would nod his head and they would turn to sand as he opened his mouth to take them all to his abaddon. No arms or weapons would save them against their only enemy, for that is what my father is to all who exist.

Watching their folly I thought them no better than grains of their sand. They could seek protection of the Creator and deny my father. That was a thought of one new to such matters. It is true the Creator could stop any act of my father. I learned humans were ever on their own. The Creator would not interfere with their choices. Thinking of why the One who made them did not serve or protect them, it was then I realized why my father had no restrictions.

There was no chain around his throat.

He played the humans knowing they had no savior to protect them. It was to his advantage and he used it ruthlessly at all times. Yet I kept thinking that if he had no chain around his throat, and I was as he as a hasataan, then I was not as he was at all.

Willing a small hovel on the edge of the new town, that night I could do no other than think of how he had no restraint but had put one on me. I Willed a call to him as I watched the candles flickering in the room full of cushions and silks. He was at first a flicker of flame, then himself sitting in the middle of the floor staring at me.

"Daughter, you have learned much for one circle of this pebble. You have learned that humans are beholding to me and are fools. I see you also learned what power you have. Did you enjoy watching the ones who had sight of you fall dead?"

Looking at me with curiosity, he was serious and wanted to know if such gave me the same pleasure it gave him. I let my burka and hijab fall and stood there naked as I wanted to hide nothing from him.

"No. It gave me no pleasure. You may see all of me, the ones here… nothing of me. To have pleasure I would need to know they were deserving of such fate."

He smiled.

"It matters not if I tell you they are all deserving of such fate. You are not here to like or dislike what you do. If you were to know one they may love you or you may love them. That cannot be. That is why I made you to be as you are to them. Doom. If they wish a look, they are already damned by their lust and they are mine."

"It is my Knowing. I answered that I did not enjoy it, that is all. I have learned something that troubles me. You have no chain on your throat but put one on me. How can I be hasataan if I am held back?"

Hearing me ask such a question angered him. He stood before me, eyes looking down into mine.

"You are not Knowing. You think I have no chain? What I have is worse than that chain of yours. I know you are new. It is only you do not know all things yet so I will forgive such a question. I will let you answer it and learn it now. On this day. Where am I from?"

"You are from the home of the Creator. What is called Heaven."

"That is so. It is a place all wish to ascend to. It is wonderful, not like abaddon. So, daughter, what is the only place I can not go?"

"Heaven, father."

"That is so. With all my power, I am not able to go to my home. Do you understand that is a chain around my throat? Worse than a chain? All here, even a worm, they have Free Will. The Father honors it for the smallest insect, but not for me. If I had Free Will,

I could go home. I have no choice. I cannot do my Will. That is why you have a chain. To be like me."

With that, he was gone. My home was love, his was Heaven. Neither could be in the only place we wanted to be. As I thought such, I heard his voice in my mind saying that was so. He added to never ask again. I thought no more as he knew my thoughts if he wished though I had no wish to know his. My mind was a calm place. His was madness.

Walking naked into the night it was different than when the Sun was above. I had never been in the Creator's darkness before. Gazing up at the stars, seeing the moon, feeling a breeze that was cool…
I thought them far better than the sands of my father's mind. I realized I was happy to be of form in such a place. Hearing a noise, I saw a shadow nearby and rose far above to not be seen as the shadow was of one approaching. Seeing me would be death and I wished no such work on that night. I rose higher until I could see the lights of the town and beyond. Like the stars above they were twinkling lights of fires, lamps and candles in thousands of dwellings. Each one held humans, and each had a story. Hopes and dreams.

Rising ever higher, I could see many human towns and places scattered in a pattern that was simple to understand. Most were near a river of water. Humans were reaching to new places, again following water. As I was high enough to see earth where it was a round globe, I was between the land below and the moon above. There were masses of land and large waters. The humans kept to the shores of the waters and lights were the shapes of the land from the sky. All I saw was the many places I would travel to take fools for my father. There were many and there was much I had to do in his stead. Like the ones below me, I too would wander the lands. They searched for shelter, water, food and safety.

I would search only for souls.

Ones Deserving Such

Know I was a phantom as I walked the market of the desert town looking for garments that would cover me and be as those worn by the human women there. Wondering why I found interest and fascination with such garb, I soon realized it was part of the feminine nature I was made with. Having to hide my form and sight of me did not mean I could not wear beautiful sheaths, burkas, robes or face veils. Not of earth, I had no knowledge of such attire but found myself drawn to silk and embroidered finery. It was not needed to allure any. Such was only for my pleasure. As I had no love, I could only give love to myself. I wished to have the garb speak to my beauty. Looking at the women of the town, they were not Angelic or seductive and none had a figure such as I was graced with. Even if the ones I passed did not see any part of me they would know they were in the presence what beauty is.

Buying such garb, I soon learned I had what was thought to be style and fashion. Each thing I bought was the most expensive item the seller offered. They would look at me with surprise saying it is most costly. I would never ask how much as I had pockets in my burka. Reaching in, I would pull out a handful of the gold stater they wished for it, hand it to them then walk away with the garb. Leaving, they called I had given too much. There was no end to the gold coins when I reached for them so they would soon tell all of the one who was in beautiful attire was generous with her blessings. It was the way to have the ones who my father craved come to find me. That was true, but my truth was I liked nice things.

Finding boys who were willing to do what I asked in exchange for stater, I had found one who was smart and not a beggar. He was good at finding things I liked. I first told him I wanted only the rarest flowers from the market each day. He asked if there was anything else that would please me and I said that I wished the rarest incense and oils that would be in harmony with the scent of the flowers. Giving him a handful of the coins, I found him wise as he would come back with things that I had asked for and he would hand me coins as all bought was less than I had given stater for. I would nod and thank him for his honesty, then say to keep what was left for his trouble. I later learned he bought food for the street children who had no home so they would not have to steal.

Knowing I could use my Will to make all such adornments appear, I found it suited my mission to be known as the one who dwelled in such finery and surrounded by the rarest of scents. One day the boy asked me why he could never see my face and with caution asked if I had been disfigured or suffered harm. It was a genuine concern. I told him that none may see me for my beauty was more than any could view and remain alive.

"You are that beautiful? A bint beyond what any may see?"

Telling him that was so, he began crying, something new to me. I knew what it was, but had never experienced it. I asked why he shed his tears.

"For you, I wish only to ask if you are bint or fata so I may address you with respect. I cannot see if you are young or grown. You are so small I think you may be bint, but what if no? I worry of it."

He was worried for my feelings and that too was something I had no Knowing of. I found I was concerned for his as well.

"Boy, you are kind. Worry not. I am neither. I am not young or old. Only beautiful. I have no imperfection to worry of."

Stopping his tears, he wiped his face then said then he would call me *She Who is Beautiful*. I smiled under my veil and told him that was much to say.

"That is a kind way to address me, but I am happy if you just call me *She*. I will know you mean me."

 Lucifer's Daughter

Bowing, he said, "Yes, She, for you, that I will do."

Knowing that the others in the town and market understood
the boy was doing my bidding, they would ask of me, and he was
honest and the next time I went to the market all there addressed
me only as *She*. In time, there would be many epithets that would
follow *She*. *She Who Must be Worshiped*. *She Who Must be Adored*.
She Who Must Never be Seen. The list grew long, and I deserved all
such descriptions as I had begun my father's work.

On my next walk through the streets at night, seeking only to
be in the breeze and see the sky, a rich man in silks adorned with
gold chains was walking with purpose towards me. He was tall
and strong, showing his muscles and they were oiled and shining
from the moon. He had a neatly trimmed beard, his eyes were
lined with paint, and there were inkings on his face in glyphs. He
carried himself as one of power and might and I knew his intent
for he had a glow around him that was a sign from my father that
I was to take him that night. It was my first take. I worried not. I
had seen the ones in the sand fall from a mere glimpse of me and
the man was no different except in garb and riches. As I looked at
him, I had Knowing that if I were not Elsa, just a woman of earth,
he would seize me and take me to fuck me for his pleasure even if
I wished it not. That alone was reason enough to take the fool.

I wished to learn of such arrogant humans and would first see
what power he thought he had over a lone woman most small.

Boldly walking up to me he said I would have pleasure that night
for he had decided to gift me his cock and give me much of it if I
proved worthy.

I stopped, froze time, and his mouth was open as he finished
the last word. I walked to him, and looked into his mouth,
wondering what was in him as I had much to learn of the humans.
I wondered if there was a serpent hiding, or something other
making him think I would not be worthy. I was the mightiest

being on the strange pebble and he was not. I circled him and
pulled at his sheath to see the cock he thought would give me
pleasure. A gift of a man to a woman. True, it was only my first
take, but I understood why my father had put a glow around his
form, telling me he was one to take. The notion that he was a gift,
better than a woman, was something not even my father thought
of himself. I was as he and he did not send a man to reap ones
such as the fool. He sent a woman. He understood the power of a
woman is equal to a man although not always of might alone. It
was meeting this first fool, hearing his sick value of women, that
made me certain he would see the power of a woman. Of beauty.

I let time return.

He stood with arms folded, waiting for me to beg such pleasure.
I wished to learn more than my own opinion so asked him if he
thought one as small as me could satisfy one so large as him. He
shook his head then reached through his sheath and pulled out his
cock for me to see.

"Thank the gods for such a kindness. Now let me see what this
shall fuck."

Obliging him, I pulled my veil up so he could see only my mouth
as I licked my lower lip. He stood, frozen, face in a state of gasp,
and his cock grew large and shot white streams my way though I
was backing away as I wore such fine silk and wished to see him
die for his arrogance. It was nothing more than him shooting
his cum, gasping for air, falling to his knees, then landing face
down in a puddle of his white cum as he stared up to me with
a pleading. I decided to unleash the power of abaddon, of the
hasataan, and I waved my hand to have all that covered me vanish.

My wrath for his notions was so strong I lit the planet as if it were
full daylight. I glowed with the light of a thousand stars for a mere
second. That was to let go of my anger, nothing more. He was
dead as I stood only showing my mouth to him. As his sad form

lay there in its finery and gold, his face shriveled as all his liquid left his entire form to produce endless cum, I saw the reaper come as his spirit rose into a spiral of sand. It was gathered and he was no more. He became nothing more than grains of sand in my father's mind and a hollow vessel now empty of spirit as I walked on.

All on Earth had awakened from the flash of abaddon's fire I had unleashed. I heard many come and they shrieked and called for Allah to show mercy, then called to warn other that *She* had been seen and that is why *She* must never be seen.

For all that, I felt nothing. I had no sympathy for the fool. He had Free Will and chose to tell me I may not be worthy of his pathetic cock. I had no respect for man who had no respect for a woman. He thought his form, one large and of might, gave him leave to take any woman he wished and use her. If I had not the power I did, I would have been carried away by him and made to do his bidding. He did not ask. He did not respect my form except for use, and what he did would affect how I would be hence.

It was my first experience of such being done to me as he thought only I was a woman. I saw much in the light I unleashed. What the fool did to me was equal to what my father did when he took a soul. He used his Will to satisfy his desires. To me, when I gave death to the man, it was fair. He was intent on taking something from me that was not his, nor was it given. In turn, I took something from him.

His existence.

Though I knew my father was evil and had treated humans in such a manner, I understood that he wished me to only gather vile creatures such as the man who lay in his cum before me. My father had never said take ones who were kind and decent, but I assumed it was only because they were full of love for the Creator and they

would not be affected in the same manner by looking at me. I had
yet to learn if that was true, but I would try showing myself to
a righteous man if I could find one and I worried that would be
hard to do.

New to the land of humans, the only one I knew to be righteous
was the boy who served me. I knew him to be honest and kind,
sharing his stater with ones in need. He had shown me the
respect and honor all who exist deserve. Though not a man,
he was still a man in his making and I worried if I revealed my
visage he would perish. I wished to find out if all were subject
to death from viewing me, or only sad fools like the man who
wished to take me.

Knowing if the boy was truly good, even if he were to die from
seeing me, I knew his being would not descend to abaddon. It
would rise to Heaven and be with the ones who were Holy in
spirit. It was a comfort to know that what the boy was in spirit
would be safe, and I wished to think on it before such a trial be
given. For this, I Willed my father to be with me on the street
where I stood looking at the fool. He appeared.

"Your first take was righteous. What did you think of the man so
full of his intent to take you?"

I saw he had stopped time. All around was standing still, and
people in the distance who were in awe of what happened were as
statues. There was no sound, no wind, no movement of any kind.

"He was like you. Thinking he could take whatever he pleased."

His eyes staring into mine, they were a question and offered no
anger or pleasure.

"Daughter, you are Knowing but not experienced. I take what
I need. Not what pleases me. Do you think this creature pleases
me?"

I nodded.

"Having his spirit to feed the sands pleases you. Do you think him worthy of respect? No. You respect none except yourself."

Raising his hand, we left the street as he Willed us to a Vision.

"Daughter, again, you are Knowing of what is, not why it is. You are right that I respect no human, but there is one I respect. This place we see is long ago and the day I fell from Heaven. All you need do is watch."

We were on a road made of sand and it was like earth, but not earth. Ahead of us was a man more beautiful than even my father so I was certain he was an Angel. He had no smile and showed no Joy. He was standing where the road changed from a barren path to where things became lush and filled with beauty. As we stood watching I knew the Angel could not see us as it was a Vision, nothing more. It was sight of what had happened already and we could not be part of it.

Wearing a simple cloth sheath tied at the waist with a cord, what caught my attention was he was crying much like the boy had done when he thought he offended me. In the cord was a thing most strange. A simple rod that could be held by his hand. I knew not its purpose, but I felt a fear in my father when seeing it. We watched as the man went from the path to a stream where there were large stones, most big as me. Not using his Will to move them, he took them one at a time using only his hands and might to the place we were looking at. When he had gathered a great number of the stones, he began placing them with skill on top of one another to form two pillars, each on one side of the road. I had no understanding of how they stayed in place as the stones began to form mighty spires in the air. He began to rise with each one to place them in a curve on each side. The two pillars eventually curved to where they met each other from each side. A last stone was placed, and I knew no Will to hold them was needed. The placement of the stones and the support each stone gave the next formed what was an arch.

Standing back to look at it, the Angel floated up to stand on top of the arch. Testing it, he found it to be solid and no stone moved. Spreading his arms wide, he stepped forward off the stone arch, floating down to the path and stood before it. It was then I understood the strange rod held in his waist cord.

Taking it, he held it in his right hand in front of him and looked at it as shaft of light shot from it into the air. It was pure power. It was light so bright it would blind any human, and it glowed and hummed. I feared it immediately, knowing my father felt the same. He stood still, arms crossed, watching the Angel intently.

Holding the light, the Angel looked down the road where we stood, then used a voice that was a trumpet that could be heard throughout all existence.

"Know this. I, Michael, love of Ethereal, father of Gloria, give warning to all fallen. I tell you this, and take heed, and forever Know…"

He took the light and tilted it down to the sand and dust of the road. He used it to draw a line in front of the arch. It etched into the path, and I was Knowing it would never be covered or fade away. He stood in the middle, and the light grew longer as it went to the sides of the road far from the middle and the line was wide as the road, wide as the arch. With that, his trumpeting words sounded once more.

"This day I draw a line in the sand. It is the line between Heaven and any of abaddon or who follow my brother Lucifer. Know that if you cross this line, you will be struck by my Blade and you will be no more. No evil shall pass for I hold this line true. To know where it is, I have built an arch over it. I, Michael, will guard the line forever for I am now the Archangel. If you are evil, know me, for I am your doom."

With all hearing his proclamation, he stood under the arch with his Blade held straight up and it was a thing all could only fear. The light of the Blade was no longer only that to carve the line in the path. Raised straight up its blaze reached to all eternity. It was a beacon, a light all evil could see, guiding them to him to be struck down if they thought they could ever harm an Angel again.

I saw my father turn away. The Vision was gone and we were back on the street with the dead form of the vile fool before us. He turned to me.

"Do not think I respect Michael's Blade. Know it is the only thing that can cast me to nothingness. I respect Michael for what he did. He drew a line that I may not cross. His Will gives the Blade it's power. He is more than Angel. He is true to himself, not the Father. He has my respect. None other. Only him."

Inside I felt a thing that was more powerful than I could comprehend. I found myself aroused. It was a feeling I long for each moment since then. I was the very lust that humans had. It was the lust my father had, though his was only for revenge. It was the need of a woman for a man. It was a power greater than anything I knew then or have known since. At the sight of Michael I wanted to be with him. My spirit longed to be in his embrace. I knew it was love. My father knew what I felt and nodded at me.

"Yes. You love Michael. There is no way you can feel other. I have told you that you can love none but me. I have said that any who love you, I will cast to nothingness. Yet, knowing you have love for Michael, I do not go to take him. Do I not speak true?"

With the feelings rising inside of me, knowing it was love for the Angel, I feared that my father would take him, then I realized the Angel was the only one who could cast him away. If my father

approached Michael, he would cease to be. I was filled with questions, then a Knowing.

"You speak true, and I know you have much planned. You gave me Vision of the Angel so the love in me would be real. You allow me to love the only one who can destroy you. The one you respect, but I know such respect is fear, and fear is your language and way. So, this is why I exist? To stop the Angel? I am temptation and even the Angel cannot resist me. When in me, fucking me, you will take him?"

He nodded.

"You created me to take the only one who can stop you from taking Heaven. I was made to one day fuck the Angel?"

He nodded.

"Father, do you think I will fuck the one I love to allow you to take him?"

He nodded.

"I know you will. He will want to fuck you. I may not enter Heaven, but daughter, you are not a fallen Angel, and nothing will stop you from passing through the arch. He needs love. You need love. It is what will happen. You will take his power and then I can enter. There is something there I must have."

All said filled me with ire. I was nothing more than what the dead fool on the ground thought me to be. A thing to fuck. Nothing more. I looked at my father in disgust, and he knew what I was thinking. I was not what he thought, and he would learn that. I had only a question.

"Why? What is there you must have to do all you have done?"

I saw him fill with sadness and longing. It was not the Lucifer any had ever seen or would ever see.

"In Heaven is the reason I fell from Grace. What I gave all for. What I must have. A girl. The girl promised to me, then denied me. My Sweetness."

Turning to look at another Vision, we both watched a young girl, just a child, playing in a field of wheat. Far behind her, harvesting the wheat with a scythe was the Glorious Michael long before he was the Archangel as he was different. Humble, not like when seeing him at the arch.

With Vision of the Angel girl, she was blonde, happy, and was the meaning of the word Joy. She was something I had no idea could exist. She was what beauty and goodness was. Then, I saw my father walking through the field, waving at the little Angel, then walking to her. He held out his hands and she put hers in his, then asking him to please make her fly. He held tight her hands and began turning in a circle, fast so that she lifted up off the ground as he went round and round. She called out she was flying as if she had wings. Finally, he slowed, and her feet went to the ground once the turning stopped. She moved to him and hugged him, thanking him for giving her wings to fly.

Michael did not interfere and it seemed to be a thing done many times before and was understood. If the Angel had walked closer he would see what I could see. The girl, only tall as my father's waist belt, had wrapped her arms around him, and as she let go I saw the large bulge under my father's sheath. His cock was fully erect, the young girl innocent of what it meant.

"Father, that is sick. You fell from Grace for that child?"

He nodded, then looked at me in a way that has been with me since.

"She was more than child. She was what I was promised. I was told, when created by Father, that the most beautiful Angel ever to exist was to be my mate. The Creator, on the day first Angels were made, created mates for all but me. When I asked where is my mate, he was confused saying he knew not other than she would come, and she would be the sweetest of all Angels. I waited, but none such was Created for me. Then, the one you saw, she was born of the first two Angels. She is the sweetest Angel for she is born pure Angel, not made by the Father. She is the sweetest of all, and I was promised she would be mine. But she never grew more than the girl you saw, happy to be a daughter. She loved me only as her uncle, but never as her love. I had been deceived."

I looked at him, stunned, thinking only why he would want one who did not love him. He knew my thoughts.

"Daughter. I wanted only what I was promised. Nothing more. When I learned that would never be, I vowed to deny my Father in the same manner. I fell, took many of his First Angels with me, and I thought one who fell, the mother of my Sweetness, would have her with as she fell. No. She was left with the Angel Michael, her father. The Archangel. The one you love. Again, I was deceived…"

It all filled me. I knew what he had decided.

"So, father, that day you became the hasataan. You vowed to hurt the Father as He had hurt you. And I am to be the one to take the Archangel so you may have your Sweetness."

He nodded, then vanished.

I watched as the dead form of the arrogant fool was gone, taken away in the wind of the gatherer, for time had returned.

I understood much. My father had worked to corrupt humans to defile all that was Holy or good. When the man came to rape me, he was acting as my father taking the girl. He thought I was his, just as my father thought the young blonde Angel girl was his.

Earth was filled with fools doing the wish of my father, taking all innocence and Joy the Creator had given them. Each man taking a girl or woman was in honor of the day my father would take the child Angel.

It was then I realized my purpose. I would reveal my sweetness to those doing his bidding and cast them to his sick mind.

Scroll VI

Boy

Know only my hope was that I could reveal myself to ones good, causing death only to those who are vile. I was young and foolish for I had existed only a short time on Earth and knew only what my sick father had given me as Knowing. He had explained that I was to take fools who could do the only thing he could never do.

Take what they wanted most.

The large brute man with such arrogance to equal my father had been able to take young virgins and defile them. That was a reminder to my father that he could not do that with his Sweetness. Each who had such ability to take what he wished was to have Vision of true lust, me, and die for it. My father knew the price to have the Angel child was to perish, so any who did what he could not do would perish to give him their Will.

Thinking he only wanted ones who did the thing he could not do, I wished to learn if I could talk to those who were good and have company in my sad job as the death of sick men for my father.

It was understandable to think that, but I had yet to learn the nature of humans fully. In time I learned that any human could be good, but also one day change to bad. No human was truly good. Many may never be influenced or drawn to my father's ways, but having Free Will, they were free to do that if it served them. It was a hard lesson. I learned it the day after my first take, the day my father showed me the Angel I was destined to fuck.

Not knowing if all would fall before me, or only the ones like my father, I decided to show boy the slightest hint of my form.

That is the day I learned my curse.

In the morning boy came into my home with beautiful flowers, smiling to see if they were pleasing to me. I nodded and told them they were most beautiful and thanked him. He stood before me waiting to be told of what else I may wish him to do.

"How else may I please She? There is much wonder in the market and knowing you wish beauty surrounding you I can find what is most pleasing for you."

He stood, smiling. He spoke true he wished to do what he said, and I wished to give him beauty in return, for I was beauty.

"Boy, you are most kind to me. Stater… know it is nothing. Just a thing you hold in your hand, nothing more. Your smile is something I value far more than gold in your hand. You give me more than I give you and I do not think that is fair."

He looked up at me, shaking his head, not agreeing with me.

"She, you give me much. I am the one here, with you. I get to be with She, and that is a gift no other has."

As I knelt in front of him, I was able to look into his eyes. They were true and had no deception. He felt being near me was gift enough and I understood it meant much to him.

"You are here because in this world of bad people, you are good. You are kind. I wish you to never fall to evil. I wish to give you a gift far beyond what can be had by any other. You know that any who are bad will fall dead from vision of me. Boy, you are good. I am not sure, but if I let you see some of me, it would be a gift that will be beyond treasure. Never having revealed myself to any who are good I worry that they may fall dead from sight of me. I can only say I know not if that would happen if I gave you that gift. I worry you may perish and that is not what I want."

Standing there, he was thinking. His eyes closed, and he was taking deep breaths.

"She. I have thought of what is offered. All around me is death. Ones younger than me are killed or raped. Most die of hunger. If I had not found She, I would soon be dead. If you leave, I will be like the others in the street. I would die with nothing more than memory of She. That is true. I know that I would like to die with sight of you. You are the only one who has been kind to me. I think that since I will die, that would be the way I wish. She, I tell you, this is my wish. I wish to see She. If I die, I die honored. If I live, I will know in this life I have your gift forever. It is your gift to give. I stand ready to take if you wish to give."

He was everything my father was not. He was brave and willing to give all to test his goodness. I knew if he were to perish he would be in the arms of an Angel. He spoke true it was better than to die in a ditch after starving or used in some sick manner by a follower of my father.

Reaching to my cheek, I pulled at my veil to reveal my face.

The smile on boy's face as he died will be with me always.

For the first time he had been given the gift of love, for that is what I knew it to be. His smile was not from sexual excitement. He was not erect nor had an orgasm. Just his smile as he attempted to thank me as he collapsed into my arms.

Then I saw his spirit rise. It was beautiful and he again smiled at me as an Angel appeared and took his hand. The Angel lifted one knee so one foot was slightly above the other, then raised her right hand into the air as the other held boy's hand. They flew upwards through the roof above and I knew the boy was in a better place than this sad home of humans. I felt tears run down my cheeks as I looked to the ground. Boy had brought me a little statue made from wood. It was crude, and I know he had carved it himself. It was of me, fully covered in burka and hijab, and at the base he had carved "Malaka."

Boy was a profit. He had carved that he saw me as Angel.

Folio II

None So Wise

Know I accepted that days turn to weeks, weeks into months, months into years, years into decades, decades into centuries then millennia, I did what my father bid me to do. Time is a human notion and meant nothing to me. Being eternal, I worried not of passings or of deaths and births. Humans were truly grains of sand that come and go as they are in the desert of existence. They fear death, never believing there is existence beyond the sad life they live for but a moment while on earth. If they believed in life eternal, life as a human would be calm and but a moment to contemplate their soul.

It is true many preached of life eternal. The clerics and holy men, the mystics and prophets all told of life beyond the one given to those on earth. Many built followings that grew large. All too soon those preaching life eternal were revealed to care only of life while on earth, taking stater and always taking the nubile young women who idolized them. All fucked their believers and found preaching reward them in endless perversions. Know that all followed my father who guided them to the sacred places — the bodies of young women. He knew that even more than stater or power, holes to fuck were valued above all else.

To all such self-created holy or wise men, I was the prize. My father let them know that I was the only fuck worth having and all sought me out.

What was most sad was they attempted to lure me into their cults or churches. Told by my father to visit this one or that one, I would say to them I may join them at my leisure, and at night I would go to their palaces where they were waiting for me. They waited surrounded by dozens of naked women offered to please me in any way I wished though they were not ones who would offer me the gift of their seed. The girls and women surrounding them were to show they were adored by such whores. Thinking them under a spell or delusion I would wave them away and feeling the power I had all would flee. The fool would take it that I wished him to myself and say so. I would nod and stand before him as he grew hard to show his offering. Most time it was not much of one, but it was all they had. They would give me permission to worship it, to kneel before them and surrender to it. I would say only I could do naught with my face covered so. I grew to prefer that they seal their own fate by coming to me, and with a smile of sinister power slowly lift my veil from where it rested on my breasts.

That was all that was needed. Seeing even my throat they gasped but the fools kept lifting as they could not stop what had started. I would watch their faces. At first so confident and assured, then their mouths open in a gaping hole, then I'd pull their hands from my veil as they began erupting in orgasm, never looking down to it, eyes locked only on me. Each had a different way of thrashing. Some died standing up, cum squirting so far as to put out candles or knock over lamps. Others bent over and with cum splashing on their faces as they gagged from it gushing into their mouths. Most fell to their knees, often holding their cocks as they made one last call to me, thanking me for what I gave. It mattered not to me. The gatherer would come, and they would be taken as harvest. They would be nothing forevermore.

Watching them such I soon began commanding the stupid girls and women to stand behind me and watch what real fucking was. The fool would delight in knowing his conquests would watch him take the one all craved to show them how powerful he was letting them know they were but mere holes while I was the most prized of all. As the ritual proceeded, being behind me none could see me, but they all saw the fool cum and go from sight of me. After the gatherer came, I would turn and all were cowering in fear, mouths open but not able to speak. I would look at each one, all of them naked, most young and fine of form. I wished to break whatever spell they were under or let them know they had made a foolish mistake.

"That is what you gave yourself to? That was what you worshiped? What now? Do you find another? Are there no loving men to have you? Know this. If I see you with some other deceiver, I will reveal myself to you and you will be taken with the fool."

Arms waving, shouts of no, never, thank you, please do not worry… they fled. I knew some would repeat the false worship, others would find a man who would love them. If I could not be loved at least the ones I warned could be if they opened their eyes. It mattered not, but I wished to see if the truth meant anything to the foolish ones who had given themselves to such sick worship. Praying to my father was sick, but praying to a disciple of my father was pathetic. It was another way to deny my father what he thought would be his. I took pleasure in taking whatever I could away from him and his minions. It was a pastime, nothing more. If they wanted to be fucked and fools for a fool, I cared not. It was ever to deny my father easy takes.

In time my father appeared, knowing what I was doing. He laughed speaking of it saying he was glad I had a pastime and hoped it amused me for it amused him.

"Father, you are more pathetic than the depraved I send to you. None are a prize. They are the scum at the bottom of a stagnant pond. That is of value? They will never ascend, only descend to you. I only wish to see how easy it is to persuade them. It takes no skill or effort. Is that your skill? Taking that which has already been given? I am trying to figure it out."

"Elsa, I have told you they are easy takes. Yes, they are destined to abaddon, but I take them early for a reason. I am sure you have considered why. Do you have thought on the reason?"

"Oh, father. I have your Knowing but do not share your perversion. I see things true. Yes, if they are not taken a true holy man may attract them and pull them from your grasp. Since they are lost, you see no need to wait. I know that."

Rubbing his chin, he shook his head then scoffed at me.

"That is simple to understand. I know you are aware there is more. What am I really doing?"

"That too is simple to know. All here began believing in a true God. With your taking the holy men, revealing them to be deceivers, you are changing all faith to disbelief. It's to deny not just the harvest, but all human faith in God. You give them earthly pleasures to deny them the Grace you lost."

Nodding, he said I was Knowing, so was not his plan working?

"Father, if you wanted such to be, then you are doing everything wrong. It is pathetic."

He pretended to look hurt, shocked I would say such of him. He asked what then should he do?

"Oh, that is something you know not? Don't deceive me, father. It can never be. This chain can pull at me, but it cannot fool me. If you wanted to corrupt all here you would appear to all. You would be the hideous hasataan in form and command them all to abaddon. You would take all, leaving nothing here for the true Father. All that you do here is a game. A taunt. You could grow large and swallow this earth and all on it. But you don't. Why, I care not. Never do I think this a mission. It is a taunt, nothing more. You are like a gnat, ever a pest. That is all."

Laughing, he was delighted.

"Elsa, you are Knowing. If I were to consume all, what would I do after such to hurt my Father? But as a pest, a gnat as you wisely call me, I am always there to remind him. But you have failed to see the real reason. I would destroy all to have the only thing I want. The taunts are not to my Father. Open your eyes. They are to my Sweetness."

I will share I had no Knowing of that. It was a thing I had no understanding of and it shook me. It was then I understood my father to be fully insidious. Understanding the young Angel would feel that all suffering was because of her, that she existed and denied him, she would have but one way to stop all pain and suffering of all in existence. All pain started the day my father fell from Heaven and created abaddon. She alone could stop all suffering by surrendering to my father. It was then I realized there was one who suffered more than my father, more than me.

Gloria, the Angel, suffered as none ever had or ever would.

She suffered the shame of being Holy. Michael, also Holy, was just in the way of my father taking Gloria. All he did was to shame her to do wrong and be with him. It was as if I were crushed by the weight of all that existed. It was so evil and cruel I could only try to comprehend the pure evil of what he had done since the fall.

"She had grown to know she is responsible for the suffering of all. She has a choice. Be mine or be the one who allows all to suffer. All of this is to make her feel shame. To come to me of her own Will to save all."

All he said was true. I had not wanted to think it such, but he was doing what he said. All evil was ever a way to have the blonde girl. To force her to him. It was disgusting. I told him such.

"Again, I say that to have one by such device is to have nothing at all. The only win is if she wanted to be yours. To force her this way? That is like my first take. The fool who wished to rape me. If I were human, he would have body, holes… but not my want or desire. He would sicken me and be hated. That is all you will have with such a plan. If you were good… Asked forgiveness for your sick mind and wished for it to heal… If you did things to make life here joyous, then you may be given her favor. You want to bring her to you by doing everything to push her away. Father. That is insane. You are truly mad. Yours is the saddest wish I can imagine."

Smiling at me, he nodded.

"Yes, I know that. I am insane. I know I have done everything to make her despise me. It doesn't matter. It will make my take of her all the better. She will have to degrade herself and give herself to such perversion. That is how I thank my Father for what he promised. His prize, his most Holy Angel, will be used and degraded. That will be what proves Him to not be Almighty. You will understand one day. It is not a lesson you have yet learned. I admire your thinking, though. You are halfway there."

Listening to him I knew there was a method to his madness. He had thought the matter through and was genius in things such. What he said was what he would continue to do. The Angel girl would pay the price for his revenge.

"Father, why not think more on this? I know you can only lose. Your prize is being hated. Once had, it will be punishment not for the Father. It will punish you."

Shrugging, he nodded once more.

"Elsa, you are right. My existence is forever fucked. That will never change. Remember when I hurt you? When I first came to you and threw sand in your mouth? My wise daughter, one who says to do no harm, what did you do when I hurt you that time?"

I could only speak true.

"I lunged at you to bite your cock off. To hurt you."

"Yes. Hurt. It makes one wish to hurt back. Hurt is the beginning of anger. And, as on that day, anger comes when hurt. It takes over. It is all there is after the hurt. Know this, then speak from that Knowing."

He dissolved with his last words. It was true I had much to know

and learn. I knew one thing. He wished me to be part of hurting
the Angel girl. She had not hurt me. She had not hurt anyone. I
had no plan to hurt her.

Civilization

Know that growing more devious my father began a new way to use humans for his plan. Taking them was not enough. He wanted more from them. A way to hurt them in ways none had imagined. It was when humans began building empires and thought themselves gods that he appeared one day and said he wished to show me what he would want of me as he enacted a new offering.

It was the time of pharaohs. With them came armies, and humans wished to be more powerful than any mortal could be. Proclaiming themselves gods, whole civilizations soon forgot the Creator or my father, the hasataan. Their lust for ever more power was not a strength. It was their greatest folly as my father delighted in their hunger as he was feeding it.

I asked him what he wished to show me. He said to cover myself and stand by his side. Lifting his hand, he Willed us to a massive chamber in a palace of the one ruling early Egypt called a pharaoh. With massive pillars of marble, drapes covering a view of the city made from silk, all items were encased in gold and it was all in tribute to a man who had proclaimed himself not only the ruler of the land, but the new god to be worshiped. His wish was followed as his army would torture and kill any who would not bow and proclaim him to be such. His power not power was from might of blade, nothing more.

As we stood in the chamber a man walked in wearing silks with gold embroidery. He wore a headpiece of gold adorned with large jewels. He may have been large and strong at one time, but I saw an old man who could hardly keep his head held straight from the weight of the crown. He said nothing to us as he walked by. He made it up the stairs of a dais then sat in a large chair called a throne by many at that time.

I asked my father why the fool paid us no heed and he said the man did not know we were there as we were not revealing our form to him yet. I looked and saw I was vapor and pure spirit. I hadn't noticed as I was occupied looking at the adornments of the chamber. My father walked to the dais, telling me to follow, then began speaking to the man.

"Rahkma, you rule but have no might. There are ones who plan to usurp you."

The man looked around, searching from where the voice came. My father spoke once more.

"There is no need to look for my voice, I am right in front of you. Can you not see me?"

The man was shaken and looked fearful.

"Are you from the dead? Stay away! I am not in a tomb. Stay away!"

"Rahkma, I am death. It is true. You have had much life, but all life ends. You are no god. You are a man, and men die. Are you ready to go where the dead go?"

My father looked at me, nodding, smiling, saying for only me to hear that such fear was wonderful to see.

"No! I command you! Be away!"

"Sad man, you command fools, not death. I do as I please. Why should I go away? What have you to offer death?"

Shaking, the pharaoh started looking around for what he had to give. My father stopped him.

"Rahkma, death has no need for things of life. Trinkets and gold are nothing to me. Nothing at all. Do you have anything that is real? What would you have if you were naked in the sand? With nothing but the wind around you. What would you offer if we were there? I will make it simple. Let us be there."

With that, my father Willed us to the vast desert where we were alone. The man was naked and laying in the sand but could now see us both. My father wore a simple black sheath, and I was in my black silk burka with my face fully covered where even my eyes could not be seen. The man stared at us saying it was delusion, he must have been poisoned, or it was a dream.

A spear appeared in my father's right hand. He held it high and cast it into the man's stomach. He wretched with pain and screamed his agony as he bled. Holding his hand above the man, he told him to stop his wailing, or another spear would finish him. Grasping the spear with both hands, the man grew quiet. My father smiled as he twisted the spear in his wound.

"Oh, mighty, powerful god of all you see. Do you still think this illusion? A dream? You are dying. What will you offer to stop the next spear?"

Eyes wide, the man was in a panic and filled with terror.

"Everything! Anything you wish. All that I have!"

My father crouched down to look the man in the eye.

"Really? What would that be? All that you have is your soul. I see nothing else. To live, to be strong once more, would you give your soul to me? Forever? For me alone and to do my bidding?"

Weak from blood pouring from him the man cried out he would give his soul to stay alive.

A scroll appeared in my father's hand. He opened it and read what was written. It was a contract. In exchange for life and the power of body he once had, he gave his soul for all eternity to the service of the hasataan and would do anything asked of him or be in the desert to die once more but in far greater pain, his soul destined to abaddon. In his other hand a quill appeared, and my father dipped it into the blood flowing from the wound in the fool's stomach, then handed it to the man.

"If you agree to my terms, you will be whole and mighty, and in my service forever. If you agree, take this quill and sign where it says your name."

That was the first time a human sold his soul.

Later I asked why not just take him. What was the point of giving the fool anything? He told me that with one such in his service he will corrupt many. Nations. All peoples. Such work was making humans to be minions in his service, and they would be his servants. I questioned why he needed fools to do what he could do with a wave of his hand. He looked at me and had a smile of delight.

"Daughter. You saw him do the unthinkable. It was such pleasure to see. I enjoyed doing it. You know I will deceive him. He will be alive and powerful, but I said nothing of being in power. His enemies will seize his throne and he will be in a prison for a long time. Long life and powerful body are his. Freedom and power are not what he asked for… well, true, I offered no such things, but he could have bargained for them."

With humans selling their souls, giving away their Free Will, my father had endless minions doing his work. He had found a way to corrupt humans where they had power to do evil on a large scale. Emperors, kings, queens, cult leaders, holy men, the rich… where once they would only be harvested, with the deal they would be in his service for a long lifetime. Doing his work, they were his surrogates as that was part of the bargain. Evil grew as never before and most all cities and religions were built and run by the damned. My father was busy making such deals as they were his pleasure. Not wanting to, I was tasked many times with guarding his prizes and being sure they held to their bargain.

One addition to his contract became that the damned were the only ones allowed my visage. I could appear to them. As they were now demon, no longer fully human, they could not die so seeing me would have no effect on them. I had grown to not want to be seen, and the ones who could now view me were ones I wished no contact with. They were no longer humans. Not fully human, not fully demon, they were remnants of their former selves hosting my father's intent. They were not worthy of my visage, and I told my father I wished not to be used in such manner and would not reveal my form. He said only that I am to do what he asked and wanted no more discussion of the matter.

Spending time with his damned I soon learned they were given his insanity as part of the bargain. The atrocities they unleashed were more than ways to feel invincible or powerful. They were ever perversions as they felt they were above all sanity.

Watching over a cult leader I learned how such bargain was fulfilling my father's wish to attract the blonde Angel to save the ones who suffered. He commented that free to do what they wished, the power granted in the bargains would give them sickness that would result in suffering as never known before. A cult leader was the first I witnessed giving such abuse. Sight of me could not stop him. He would only be taken when my father called the due on the contract.

Having a large church of followers, they were young girls, and the men were old and rich. The leader, Jahnad, was once poor and lived alone in the desert. Bitten by a scorpion he ran to a town nearby where all dismissed him as dead as the poison had been in him long. Though filled with poison he did not die. Having survived, he found people were in awe of him for such. Each day he would go to the desert, find a scorpion, put it in a small box then return to town. In the middle of the market where all would gather, he would take the scorpion out of the box and put it on his face and taunt it. Each day he was bitten, and the scorpion would die after it stung him. News spread throughout the land of the one who could survive death and had power over the scorpions.

Soon he had followers seeking the way to be like him. He soon
knew his unusual ability attracted the weak of mind… and many
young women who wished to gain his attention. More and more
came each day. All gave him their stater, the girls giving him their
bodies thinking his power would flow into them. He built a large
church that worshiped the scorpion and at service each day he
would be bitten by ones caught for him by followers. He proclaimed
that he could give the might of the scorpion to a young woman who
needed such power. He would choose the most beautiful one there.
He would call the young girl to the front of the congregation and lay
her on the alter naked, then would straddle over her, his cock just
above her mouth, telling all that just like the scorpion he was using
his stinger on the girl. Taking a scorpion, he would hold it over his
tongue, and it would sting him. As it did so he pushed his cock into
the girl's mouth and as she sucked it he would cum in her mouth
and cry out the sting of the scorpion had flowed through him and
was now in the girl. All would shout praises and the girl would keep
sucking him until the cries quieted as he moved from her mouth to
put his cock in her to fuck her, saying he was unleashing his own
might against the scorpion into the girl so she would survive. He
fucked her until he came in her and she shouted out she was alive.
The followers were driven to a frenzy, all women there asking to be
next. Saying he still had more to offer, he would fuck women lined
up until he could no longer cum.

Once making the bargain with my father he took such vile use
of girls to worse depths. He would fuck them first, then to prove
if they were worthy, would take scorpions from a box and place
them on the girls to sting them. All but a few survived and he
proclaimed they were not true believers. Each day one would live
while a dozen or more died. The ones who did survive were all
stung by scorpions provided as part of the bargain from my father
as their sting held no poison. The fool Jahnad had no memory of
the bargain terms, and believed his own story as did his followers.
Soon, all believed that if fucked by Jahnad they were immune to

the sting of scorpions. They were sent to the desert to spread the word. Not expected to return as they were spreading his word, the truth was the desert was filled with the dead bodies of young girls bitten by potent scorpions, swallowed by sand for the gatherer to find and take as harvest.

I was sent to him when he closed the church one day. He had a thousand young women, all beautiful, all devoted to him, gathered there. He had grown tired of the ceremony and wished only to fuck them without interruption and stopped sending them out to the desert to seek converts. I was sent to take Jahnad. He had violated the contract. His soul came due.

Willing myself to his church, as I entered I saw near a thousand young women, all naked, all pleading to be fucked by him. His desires had grown ever more perverse, and he was torturing three at the alter as they hung from chains. He was slashing them with a spear and drinking their blood. As I walked the women made way for me forming a path to him at the alter. I was covered fully in black, and hearing quiet fill his church he looked out and saw me. He was soaked red from blood, blathering incantations that had no language or meaning. He stopped and looked at me as I walked up to him, then he chastised me for being clothed and demanding I be naked to respect him. My father, the only one who could take the due of a contract, stood invisible behind me. He wished to see the one so arrogant that he was attractive to woman fall as he called the due.

I lifted my veil and he died without orgasm. For him I did more than show my lip or jaw. I pulled the veil up to reveal my full face. The impact of such gave instant death. I stood, the veil not hiding my face. It hadn't mattered if the ones hanging from the chains looked my way for they were already dead. I saw the gatherer come and take the harvest, adding the three hanging there. I Willed myself back to my home. I was Knowing if this was the first of the damned to break the terms, the ones next would be worse and more perverse than Jahnad.

They were.

Watching humanity grow in number, cities forming, rulers acquiring wealth and might, the ones taking the deal from my father grew in number and he empowered their sickness. Many wanted only long life and power, but there were also many who wanted sexual prowess for perversion and to be free to do what they wanted with none able to stop them. My father was certain that they were the best deals he made as they offended the true Father most. Perversion always preyed upon innocent humans. They were the fodder for such fools. All deals hurt not the one selling their soul, they hurt the people they ruled or had power over.

Know that although I am the meaning of lust and desire, beauty and attraction beyond all humans, it does not mean I am like humans and have acceptance of perversion. The beauty I have was given to me, and I would not surrender my soul for it or any form of sex. I have learned, more than any human ever will, that sex is meaningless when not given or taken in a state of Union. It is a manifestation of love within. Without, it is just a physical act that lasts but a moment and is gone. I have never been tempted by physical desire, nor shall I ever be. It is true a human may hear me say such, thinking that is because I have such beauty and can have any sex or with anyone I want. I understand their thinking that. I have thought of what if I were deformed and hideous with none attracted to me. Would I think the same?

Know this. With the beauty I have, it is not seen by any worthy of love. I am as disfigured as the worst leper. I am but a sheath of black cloth that has to hide as all would suffer from my visage. Like a leper, I am an outcast who must shroud myself and never be seen. I have no chance to be attractive to anyone good of heart or mind. There are none who can come close and raise my veil. I am alone, and I am without love, a mate, or a friend. I am the ultimate leper for my disease will last beyond all human lifetimes. I long for a time where I may rid myself of my shroud and be a woman who can walk down a street and be met with smiles, not fear.

Even boy, one so sweet and kind, one without any bad, died from a mere glimpse of me. I know I will meet with him as I seem destined to visit Heaven at some point, and there I will be free to talk to him and reveal that I am not *She*, I am his friend. I long for such, but now I long to have escape from the task of taking the ones who sold their souls for I must visit them and see their sick worlds my father granted them.

I am not sent to ones who bargained for long life and power. Those do not hurt the true Father as much as the ones who gave soul for sexual power. Those are the ones that offend the most, and my father delights in them facing the only one not victim to their sick perversions. The one who is immune to whatever sick attraction or power my father gave them. He does not reveal himself, but he is always there to watch the expression on their face when they realize they have no power at all. It was only something they had in exchange for eternal servitude as a minion of my father. He values them after life as they are vile and make the cruelest minions when they return to earth to act in his stead.

I have come to know that the ones such fall into three groups of perversion. It is fair to say all are bad, but that can only be said by one who has never witnessed the depravity humans can reach as I have. They are what happens when, like my father, they abandon the love of the true Father. Without His Grace, they grow sick for they will never be worthy of love. If the true Father offers no love, no human will. It is not known, but that is what is. I know it, and sadly, my sick father knows it.

Looking at the first group of perversions, one may think them only gluttons for fornication. That may be a way to see it, but that is a human reaction, knot a Knowing one. I call them gluttons, and that is a fair naming. Most often men, there are many who are women. Most are truly repulsive in form and nature. Fat men, slobbish, drooling and eating endlessly, lusting after ones who are in care of their form as they are not. They wish to have what they lack. Beauty. The women are much the same. Most are obese, many old, no man or woman is attracted to them. They adorn themselves in attire and jewels to look beautiful but that makes them even more repulsive. A bloated, stinking wrinkled woman or man covered in silks, gold and jewels is horrific to view. I do not understand fully why the ones who are most offensive in form want sex only from ones most perfect in beauty. They do nothing to deserve such fine flesh, and inside they think they are the same as the ones they lust for.

Such gluttons make a bargain to be beautiful in form and have all they wish to adore them and have sex with them. In the early days of such deals my father would bid me come witness the fools. I would be of spirit, not form, and watch. My first witness was to a man that was so obese he could not stand on his own. When sitting the fat on his front and sides reached the floor and lay in rolls. Servants stood at his side feeding him constantly, the drippings of fat from roasted animal flesh dripping down his endless layers of fat to form puddles of grease on the floor. He could not rise to shit or piss, so under him were bowls filling with putrid excrement and two servants to keep emptying the bowls. It was beyond what even I thought a human could become. He was a monster of self-loathing. He hated himself and took a form all others would hate.

I wondered what the man had that my father would offer a deal to have for his use. The man was the son of a ruthless king who had died long ago, and he had inherited the kingdom. He had wealth and power, and his kingdom was worshiping the true Father. I understood that my father wished him to change such devotion. By empowering the fool, faith in the Creator would change to faith based only on fear of death. I will tell that my father is not only the ultimate deceiver, but he is also the master of making a deal. He is convincing, charming, acts empathetic, and drives a hard bargain. I learned his skill on that visit to the glutton.

"Mighty ruler of this holy land, I have heard your call. Your prayer went not to the God of your people, it was heard by me. You were

     Lucifer's Daughter

most sincere saying you would give anything to be a man of might like your father. Tall, muscular, fit as no other, handsome and virile. Did I hear your prayer the way it was meant?"

Biting a leg of some lamb, holding the bone, he mumbled his prayer was heard correctly. My father was just beginning to structure the deal.

"It is a good prayer to wish for such might. As ruler of this land, you would be respected not only as king, but as a man like no other. One all women would crave to have in their bodies. You would be lusted for by all the most beautiful women… oh, and not for the power you have as ruler, but because you would be the one with the largest cock and the mightiest fuck any have ever known. Speak true, is that the real reason for your wish to be such?"

Throwing the leg of lamb down, he looked at my father and with a desire that was as fire, said that was the reason. My father nodded and bowed.

"That is the wisdom of a true king. To know what is the real wish behind the wish. Most wise, and a wish most prized for what is to have power if not to fuck all beauties? A mighty body would not even need be king for all would want it. I must ask before we speak more if you are true in what you offered in exchange. I heard you say you would give anything to be such a man. Is that true?"

With the grease still running down his face, he said that is what he said, and that is what was true. My father smiled, then asked him who his prayer was given to. The man laughed as much as he could through his mouth almost shut fully by endless chins beneath it.

"I stopped praying to God long ago. He never answered my prayers. My prayer was to the dark lord, Lucifer."

Watching my father smile at his words is impossible to understand if not me. He was ecstatic and filled with power hearing that the man prayed to him, not the true God. It showed on his face, and he looked as if the Angel he once was as he answered.

"And I heard your prayer. I answer prayers, your people's God does not for he has abandoned them. Hearing your prayer, I am here to answer it. I can offer you what you wish. I will make you tall, mighty, have the most powerful cock of all men here, and all women will fuck you or do anything you tell them to. You will be mighty as king and lead great battles as you will be the strongest and most feared of all warriors. I offer that. Is that all you wish?"

Struggling to lean forward to look my father in the eye, he did not manage it, but cried yes over and over. My father smiled to where I was first, then to the king.

"All that I offered. Nothing more?"

Leaning back, the man said that was all he wished for or needed. I knew my father smiled at me as the man had left much out of the bargain such as a long life, health, that he be loved, that no other could usurp his power. He was so lost in his fat he was blinded to all the things that made having a fine body needed. The most impressive part was my father was being fair. He asked was there anything more and the man had a chance to ask for those things but didn't. Then my father told what the king must offer in exchange for what would be given. He reached behind his back and brought forward a scroll and opened it to show the king.

"I have heard you, and all that you have asked for is now written on this scroll. That is what I will give. Now, to give what you ask, I ask for what I want in return. This is a deal, king. A bargain. Do you understand? Yes, your nod is enough for me to proceed. Let me read right from the contract. Oh, my request is simple enough. For all you ask, I, Lucifer, ask the following in return. You will defile all virgins and have them pledge love to me, not God. If they are not sincere in their devotion to me, they will be executed.

As king, you will declare there is no God, that such deity was a lie told by your father to give false hope, and that the faith of all must be to me, Lucifer, to be known as the Lord of this life. All houses of worship will pray only to me, all symbols of faith be to me. As king, any who deny me or found worshiping any other god will be executed in an offering to me. Oh… yes. One more clause. It states that for all the above consideration, your immortal soul will be mine forever, and you will do my bidding in this life and the life beyond. It's a simple agreement. You get what you want, I get your devotion without fail, and your soul. So, are there any questions? Do you understand the terms and agree to them?"

Again, my father was precise and careful to make it a choice. If the fool said no, he would strike him down and shake his head at what sad fools humans be. The king said he agreed, and he would sign the paper. A quill appeared in my father's hand, and it was sharp. He pierced the hand of the king to let blood flow, dipped the quill in it and put it in the right hand of the man. Holding the scroll exactly where the king could scribble his name, after looking at it, my father rolled it up, and from his finger red wax dripped to seal the scroll… to seal the deal as it became known. He pressed his thumb into the hot wax and when lifted, it was not a thumbprint, it was a trident. He put it behind his back and it vanished to his collection of deals in his den in abaddon, then bid me to appear. I became visible, and he introduced me.

"King, this is Elsa. She is my daughter and will be the one to assure you follow the terms of the contract. She is as powerful as me, so do not let her small form fool you. She is your doom if you do not as agreed. Now that all the details have been attended to, I will honor my part of the contract…"

I watched as the king's fat melted off his form. It formed large pools of stench, a reminder of what the man had done to himself. It took only a short time but soon the king was standing. He was tall, had massive muscles, was handsome and had a cock that hung down to his knees. Although the chamber had no mirrors, my father Willed one to be before the king. It was tall and his whole form could be seen. The king was staring in awe, thanking my father over and over. Then my father bid him to call for his most lovely servant girl and see if she would desire his cock. Smiling, the king called out a name and a beautiful young girl entered with her head down in respect. I knew it was not respect for it was not to see the vile fat king. He commanded her to look at him for he had been graced with a new body. She looked up and her face was one of shock, awe, and desire. My father said to ask her to serve him. The king walked up to her, and she could only stare at his cock. He looked at my father and me, my father nodding to him to act. He was what he had bargained for, so spoke to the girl not in a command, but as a lover would.

"Trena, I offer you my cock. Take it and enjoy."

The girl knelt, marveling at it. She took both hands and held it, then began kissing it up and down, then it grew large and it was so big she hugged it tight to her. He told her to suck on it, and we watched as he had his cock sucked for the first time. It was so large she could barely fit the head in her mouth, but he was so excited he came from the sight, filling her mouth then pulling back to cover her face in his white stuff. Still hard, he bid her to stand and bend over. He reached inside her and began loosening her to be able to take his mighty staff. He shook and trembled as his cock went in her, hearing her cries of pain for it was so large. Soon he was thrusting in and out of her, then pulling her up, she rode on him as if sitting on a railing. He walked with her impaled on his cock and approached my father and me, proud of his first fuck. We could see a bulge in the girls stomach where it was filling her. He said he was grateful and bid the girl to bend over and suck on my father's cock, which she did. Filled at both ends, the girl was like a hog on a skewer over a fire.

"Is this what you wished for, king?"

The king grunted a yes, and my father looked at me with his sick smile to tell me to watch for the king was in for a surprise.

"It is a fine treat. This girl is most pleasing. But as you are to do my bidding, pull away for I wish to have her to myself. There are endless more for you, so worry not."

Wishing only to please my father, he pulled out of the girl and let her kneel before my father as she took him deeper and fully into her throat. My father let his cock change to serpent, telling the girl he was going to show her what a real cock was, so to pull away and watch.

With spit running down her face, she marveled watching my father's serpent appear. It grew large and soon it was wrapping around her, the head of the serpent going to her face and looking her in the eye. It's forked tongue came out and went into her mouth, and she began sucking it with pleasure. She was hugging it wrapped around her, moaning with delight as she came over and over. The king watched and I could see his expression was one changed to anger and envy. When my father was certain he had seen what real power was, the serpent recoiled and was once again his cock. He put the girls mouth over it and filled her with his cum for near an hour as she gulped it down, never letting a drop hit the ground.

The king stood frozen, clearly enraged. When my father offered her the last of his cum, he took the girl by the hand for her to stand, then kissed her. He smiled at her.

"Trena. You are beautiful and know what to do with a cock. You have had two this day. Which do you think pleased you most?"

She looked only at my father.

"Oh, yours, my lord. I will pray to have it again. I will worship only it."

He looked at the king after telling the girl he may visit her if she told all the women of the land who was the one to crave, the one to beg cock from for surely the king had little to offer. She bowed and promised she would tell all of his cock and for all to pray for it. He sent her away, then turned to the king.

"Oh, fool, don't look so angry. Your little pecker there is fine. I am sure it will get much attention. Know this. Never think you are powerful in any way. All power you have is given by me, and I will take it back if you do not my bidding. Know this and enjoy it while you are still here. As agreed to, tell all to worship me, never you. I have told the girl to spread the word that worship to me is now the law of the land, but more than law as I give pleasure more than any sad fat king who sold his soul."

With that, he vanished. The king stood, stunned, holding his limp cock, looking to me. I approached him.

"Mortal. Accept that you are a fool. You didn't ask to be the only cock craved. You only asked for what you now have. Do as Lucifer wishes and you will enjoy the sad women here. If not, I will visit you and you will fuck yourself with that twig in hell."

The king did not last long. As soon as he changed all worship in his domain, he told one slave girl to pray to his cock. That was not prayer to my father. With that, my father gave me Vision and said to take the king. I Willed myself to his chamber and he trembled with fear seeing me, saying no over and over. I sent the fool girl away, and with no other in the chamber had no wish to see the fool. I waved my hand in front of my face and showed him my beauty. He fell dead without climax. The gatherer came and he was in abaddon doing deeds not even I wish to tell.

Next are the fools who wish only control over others as a master. Know that they have none of the qualities a true master must possess. Even my father is a false master, using only might to impose his will on ones who wish to be slaves. Though he knows such, he revels in the ones who will sell their soul to have sex

slaves. As I learned the language over time, it is said such ones
are inadequate and weak. To feel strong they use sex and find
submissive ones who need a master in some way. That is sad
for a submissive needs a true master who serves them, not the
submissive serving the master. This is not understood by any but
ones truly paired, and again, my father plays off the sadness of
such weak souls. I have spoken to him of the matter many times,
and he has been certain that no human can be master, that all
humans are but slaves. His deal to the most weak is simply to
be strong and have slaves who will serve as nothing more than a
submissive hole. I will not say more as there is little to say but they
are empowered such but know they have such power only by a
lifetime of being a slave to my father. Once taken, they will be but
fuck holes doing what ones even weaker than they demand. The
price paid is to be a sex slave to the most depraved denizens
of abaddon.

Know the last group is one to be feared. They are ones, also weak
of body and mind, who wish to inflict suffering on others and
derive sexual pleasure from it. They are ones already fully mad who
will do anything to anyone and gain climax seeing them suffer.
Their acts are beyond most imaginations. I have been witness to
things that no human will want to know. All hear stories of ones
who do unspeakable things. Cannibals, sadists, hunting humans
for sport, caging people to live in their own filth, inflicting
tortures, impaling, decapitating and things I will not say for I wish
to give none such ideas of what can be done.

Though most think such people are insane, true they follow in my
father's madness, but their acts are always to have an orgasm. They
are so corrupt the only sexual pleasure they can find is from the
suffering of others. They grow ever more in need of excitement.
A mad man of this nature will only grow erect from seeing pain
and suffering. This is not a person made in the image of the True
Father. They are ones who my father took early in some manner
or were so pathetic in nature that they walked down the path of
doom. Telling my father that it should be he who reaped such

mad takes, he said there was no need to harvest. They would do so on their own. As he granted them power to do their vile acts to others, he gave them such that in time not even their evil acts gave them pleasure. I asked when all human pain no longer gave them anything, what happened then? He smiled, amazed I had so much to learn of humans.

"Daughter. Visit such fools and learn. I am not going to tell you what you should know. I have one now who is ready to harvest himself. Go there, then you will answer your own question."

With that, I was Willed to a dark cave lit by torches. I remained as spirit and could not be seen as I was there to view, not to take the fool. I walked down a long entry to the cavern and on the way found parts torn from human bodies, all ripped from them, none cut. As I entered the large cavern, the place had iron pillars with chains and straps, and torsos hung from most, none of them having heads. There was only one living in the cavern, and it was a small man who looked like one who cleaned hovels or sold dead birds. He was small of frame and feature and looked crazed and wild of eyes. He was naked and looking to the bodies for anything to fuck, but none aroused him. He began screaming to my father that he could not get hard, and he needed to grow hard and cum. Hearing no answer, I saw the desperation on his face. Shaking, his body was pathetic and looked like a skeleton. He kept crying out to my father, and he was thrashing about, flailing, throwing himself on the body parts all around him, but still his cock was hard to even see as it was small and had no erection.

Then, in the air, a leather strap floated in front of him, a gift from my father. His eyes grew wide as he took it. Tying one end around his neck he leaned backwards, choking himself while still footed on the cavern ground. I saw that his choking himself made him hard — but not hard enough. He had tortured all there and now he was going to do the ultimate act of harm. He would find orgasm by choking himself. He let himself slump down, stroking himself, smiling as it aroused him so. Finally, holding his cock, he hung there. As he choked, he kept stroking himself and he came as he died. His pleasure was from such, and I understood they would harvest themselves as no amount of perversion would satisfy them except performing such acts on themselves. He was taken by the gatherer, along with all the bodies in disarray there.

In the empty cavern my father appeared before me. I shook my head, nothing more. He looked at me and said no man is happy until a man dies. Then he vanished and I was back in my home. I was tired of seeing only such madness, and knew it was my father's way of showing me that humans were worthy of no care or love. By God, by each other, and certainly not us. It would have been easy to fall for his teaching, but I did not. If only to defy him, I thought only that with so many people there would be such sickness, but there would also be love. Most ascended to Heaven, and that meant that humans were also good and true. In my head I heard my father's voice.

"You are young and foolish. Starve any creature long enough and they will do anything to feed."

True, that was the nature of animals and wild creatures, and there were humans same as those, but humans were spirit and not creatures in the wild. I spoke back to my father.

"I am glad to be young and foolish as it is not being blind and unable to see."

He had no more to say. I spoke true that I had my own mind on matters. He could chain me but not hold my thoughts. I was not some take. I made no bargain with him. He was not my master. I was imprisoned by him but counted myself as free as I did not think what he thought.

Scroll IX
The One Sent

Know I had parted ways with my father's madness. My father decided to test me and teach me I was not Knowing. He sent his first harvester of women of Earth to Thebes, the city I dwelt and found sparse solace being there. I was Knowing that his harvester sent to influence me and to provide me with the Ritual of the Fall.

Not having a friend nor anyone who understood I was hasataan, not woman of earth, I welcomed one to talk to and speak of being a stranger in such a strange land.

Sending a harvester to Thebes made sense as the city was growing and it was the center of what some called civilization, though my experiences could not allow me to think of humans as civil. In the new center of culture and riches city were endless women who had degraded themselves and lost faith and were the ones my father wished to take. The one sent harvested only such sad women and he had been on earth long before I was created. He was once an Angel, first fallen, who fell from Grace with my father. He proved his loyalty to him and knew my father needed strength of eating souls. He was the first to leave abaddon in the service of my father and had been on earth since. I thought I could learn of events before I was created by knowing the fallen one. I thought him the worst of fools as he chose to leave Heaven and even my father thought admitted such was a foolish choice.

He was not as expected. He did not Will himself to my home. He stood outside and knocked on my door, saying he was sent by my father. Knowing that he harvested women I did consider he would think me just a woman but then decided to wait and learn if that was so. I considered his view of women must be perverted from harvesting them for so long. I do not recall him even being mentioned by my father or present the rare times I was in my father's chambers beneath the abaddon of the taken.

Opening the door, he was kind looking and handsome, but not using those traits it in any manner. He had long hair, gentle blue eyes, and a sincere look as he gazed into my eyes. I saw both his form and spirit, though I did not reveal more than form to him that day. He waited, seeing me fully covered in silk, said no more, patiently waiting for my invitation to enter. Stepping back, I moved aside and turned my head as invitation to enter and he smiled softly as he walked in. I knew he was demon true and would not be taken by sight of me. Pointing to cushions, he went to them, nodded, then sat cross-legged on one looking up to me, waiting for me to lead the way. I thought him a properly trained pet, nothing more. My father had certainly advised him that I could cast him to eternity if he was rude and it is true I would.

I decided to show myself, a thing I had longed to do.

Looking at him, I began by taking off my face veil, then the full head covering, leaving only my burka. He did not drop dead, so he was indeed a demon. Showing respect, he nodded thanks for such privilege. He was the first one to see me in such manner and I waited for him to react to how I looked.

"Do you see me as harvest? One to take?"

He shook his head from side to side, surprise showing on his face, and it was genuine.

"No. I think it would be the other way around. You are hasataan and have the power, not me. I am here as friend, that is all. I am like you. Alone here. I am happy to have one here who knows such burden."

Looking at him I saw no indication he was being deceptive, but I had no interest in being friends with any foolish as a fallen one.

"What is your name, harvester?"

He looked at me and nodded. He could tell I did not respect his role in matters.

"The Father gave me the name Michael. It was in honor of the true Michael, the First Angel. Your father gave me a name not of Heaven. Scorpio."

Such a name was more than a name. It had meaning. I wished to know why he was given such name and asked him of it.

"The day of the fall… in the blackness there… I felt a thing crawling on my leg. I grabbed it. It was then that the First Angel appeared and lit the pit with his Blade. Your father looked at me holding a scorpion. Knowing it meant harm, I ate it. From then your father has only called me Scorpio. It is a strange name for me, but there it is."

Knowing nothing other than his story, I had Knowing there was more, but time would reveal all. I decided not to leave it at his lame explanation and asked more.

"Could you not tell him you are Michael, not some insect you knew not what else to do with?"

I watched as he shook his head, almost about to laugh but restraining himself.

"I know you were not there, and I share this as one who was. Your father is not one to defy. At least not from ones such as me. I speak true and what I feel is shared by many of the fallen. On that day I was no longer Michael. No longer Angel as before. It made sense to leave my name behind as all I had been was no more. So, I am Scorpio now. Call me Michael if you wish. Just know that Angel Michael is no more."

"Then I will respect that. I will know you as demon no longer Angel. I will speak true to you. I have no regard for what you are or do. A harvester? That is sad purpose. You have lost more than Heaven. You have fallen lower than abaddon. Have you no respect for yourself?"

He looked at me with honesty. His eyes were true, as was his manner.

"Some think there is a place that is bottom. It is a comfort for most to think there is a place where nothing worse can exist. Abaddon is thought of as rock bottom. I know that is not so. There is no bottom. No depths to which one can sink. Yes, I have sunk lower than any can know. Well, except you as you speak true."

Amazed I saw him honest and sincere; I knew that was also how takes thought of my father. I saw Scorpio as evil. He idolized my father and followed his ways in making lies appear as truths. That is done by deceiving oneself. He believed all he said and why he appeared to speak true.

"Scorpio, you were foolish enough to fall. Now foolish enough to put yourself in service to my father. Know you are less than nothing to me. I think only that. I know you are still spirit and one day you may find a way to rise. I will not blame you for my father is very compelling to the weak, just as you are to the women here. Know this. Never speak to me as you do to women here."

He stared at me.

"No. I will never treat you other than what you are. You are not like ones here. I am not here to watch what you do or act in the stead of your father. Do you believe me?"

Rising off the ground, I rose above him, looking down at him.

"I believe nothing. You are nothing so I believe you not. If you do my father's wish to tell him of me, then tell him I said to go fuck himself. No others will."

With that, he broke out laughing and I could not help but join him. He gathered some resolve as he spoke to me.

"That I will take joy in telling him for it reflects my own sentiments. I am here as friend. Nothing more. This is a lonely place for one who had been in Heaven. This land has no true Grace, nor even true evil. It is just a place where none know what to do. I think you know that."

He was growing relaxed and that was what I wished so I could see him true. He had spoke the same as what I knew, and only one such as he could know that. It was good for him to say what he thought. I lowered myself and sat on a cushion across from him. I asked if he knew my name, or anything of me.

"You are what else a hasataan wished, so you are Elsa. I do not think of it other than a pretty name. I do know you are not of abaddon and not of Heaven. You are the Will of Lucifer. His spawn. I know no other way to say it. He has not shared other than you are the next hasataan and here to learn his ways."

Seeing him look at the serpent around my neck I was sure he was Knowing of it. I doubted my father sent him without reason or understanding that love was forbidden. Not having restrained myself in speaking with him, I asked what my father expected of him.

"Harvester… What has my father told you of me? What has my father asked of you in being here? Is it to take a foolish woman, or tempt me in some sad way?"

"You wish to know if I speak true? I am not foolish. No matter, as I would speak true no matter what."

He looked so sincere and innocent, I could see why he was the one who took women. I also knew that what he said was not fully true.

"Harvester, my father is an inspiration to you for you speak true not true. With me, know to speak true no matter what. So, when you take a woman, do you deceive her with talk of love, or do you say you are sending her to abaddon?"

He stared at me. It was a look of respect. I am Knowing when ones speaks true or speaks lies. I knew nothing of harvesting in the manner he did such, but I doubted he told the ones he harvested the truth that he was their doom. I watched him carefully and he remained calm and certain.

"I say nothing. I do not say I want them. I do not say they are destined to doom. That would prolong things. If asked, I would answer but the take would be the same. If you wish to understand, I will explain all there is to know. Know they are women already destined to abaddon. They have never given any their love. They were never desired. I could just look at them and call the gatherer and they would be gone. I am not cruel and I know they should have a moment of pleasure before that. So, I invite them in, stare into their eyes, and they kneel and suck my cock. I always cum in them. As they swallow, they are taken. In this life at least they had that."

Ire rose in me. He was giving them a memory of something they would not have once in abaddon. To give such, then deny them attention forever was cruel, yet he said it was not. I wished not to challenge his practice, but I could share what I thought of it.

"You give them the thing they will have no more forever. I think that is cruel. You do not?"

As I watched him, I was certain he had never thought of such. I wondered if it was he who needed such a moment. A need to be adored and wanted. I would hear his thoughts of what I asked.

"Elsa, you are new here. Even so, how can you not see what a sad life this is? I don't tear families apart or harvest ones who have love. To be desired, even if for that moment? I think it is a kindness."

Having Vision of him taking women, he was gentle and caring in manner, yet I wondered more if the moment was for him. Watching him in the Vision, he had made his lair lush and exotic. It was filled with statues of naked woman performing sex acts on men, plants all green and dark, chimes were ringing from a small breeze of his Will, and it was lit by one candle, large as him in height and having several wicks burning to light him in a flattering way. The candle said much about him, and it was a symbol of his might. It was a trap, a place to send women into a trance. I knew he was gentle, but a trap it remained.

"Candle burner, you are naught but the spider in a web waiting for fools to be attracted to your lair. You never earn their admiration or offer any love. My Vision saw true that you smiled as you came and did not even nod or wave to them as they were ushered away. I care not but know this. Nothing you do is admired by me. I am not impressed. Have you no pride?"

It was certain my words cut him as if a knife, and I wished to see him not as a demon, but as spirit. How low can one once Angel fall? I asked him, again, what had my father told him of me and was he instructed to do anything in any way to me.

"All you said is true. I have no pride. I exist. The takes are a moment of being desired and wanted and it is true I look pleased as they are pulled away. Can you understand that I feel even more alone with each one? The women who crave me? Show me any desire? Elsa, they are taken from me each time. I was once mated when Angel, but now I am alone. I say only that I wish it were real, not a harvest. Sometimes, not always. Some disgust me, but some… they are just lost or have been cast away and I see them as worthy of better treatment. Oh, and Elsa? Candle burner? You called me a candle burner. What is that?"

I shook my head. He was pathetic. If the ones before him were as he said, even if but one, he could stop the take. Have her rise up and talk to her, ask of her feelings. The story was true not true. He was alone and sad but did nothing to change it. I told him when I think of him, I see him having to light a candle to be seen in a good light. He started to laugh at the name but thought of what I said and knew it true.

"You asked of your father and what he has said to me. Know this, I speak true. He has said only that I can not love you and to keep you from loving me. He said no harm would come to you if that should be, but I would be taken not by gatherer, but by him. He would make me suffer before cast to nothingness. That was all. He said I was not here to seek pleasure. That is why I do not lift a kind, lost woman and look at her to say that like her, I am lonely and wish for love. Your father has made it certain that I would be a harvester no longer. I think we are both bound here to be without love or even hope. I heard nothing of not being a friend. In this land where we are alone among so many, I wish a friend. I offer my friendship but that is all it can be."

Hearing no deception, I understood that being alone was the sadness of both of us. I already felt the need to have a friend. I had cravings. I had watched many fuck. I could not have such though I wished it. It was not a thought, it was what was inside of me. I asked him how demons satisfy such craving, a need so strong.

"Well, I am not sure your father would keep us from the Ritual. It is not one of love. It is pure demon sex and nothing more. It is in tribute to your father to give him our devotion."

That interested me, but I was not going to give my father my devotion. If it allowed the candle burner to do such and to soothe the desire of my form, it was worth learning of. I asked him to explain the Ritual.

"It is not a human act. No human could survive it. You came long after the fall. On that day your father transformed into the hasataan and from him grew the serpent. It grew large and it found Ethereal, the wife of Michael the First Angel. He had thought she would fall with him and take her daughter with, but she deceived him. In rage, his serpent impaled her and her soul was taken. He ignited in flames for all there to see and sent his serpent to lick the cocks of all males there. All male demons now have a serpent. It is not powerful like his, but it is in his honor and grows when needed. Do you know of all I have said?"

Nodding, I knew much of the serpent but knew not of the events he described. It fit with my father's rage for not having his Sweetness that day. I said I had knowledge of the serpent, but what of tribute to it?

"It is a recreation of his serpent impaling Ethereal. If we were to enact the ritual, we would stand in darkness… maybe one small candle burning. Please, call me candle burner if you must as I would light the candle. It is fitting you named me that not knowing the Ritual. You are hasataan, that is true. We would be naked and you would act as Ethereal. You would stand before me, and instead of deceiving him, you would worship him. You would find a vial of sacred oil — the scent she had when Angel — in your hand. I would stand and you would pour the oil on me, rubbing it over all my places, then rub yourself on me to share the oil entirely on your form. We would shine from the oil, and you would stand in front of me, stare up to me in adoration just as he wished Ethereal and her daughter should have done. My cock would change to serpent and it would grow large to circle you many times. You would caress it, hold it tight and ride it as it goes up and down. It would lift you up in the air, and then you would collapse, falling back, the serpent entering your bottom then coming up out of your mouth and you would hang limp in the air fully engulfed and know the power of the serpent. Then, I would have the serpent bring your face to mine and we would be in embrace. The passion and intensity would recreate the fire of his form when he became the burning monster hasataan and we would ignite in flame, the oil being what burns, not our forms. We would each cum from the fire and that is what is tribute to your father. It is for his pleasure… to have him know we think what he did was glorious, and we pay tribute to it."

I nodded for I had Vision of it as he told of it. It was not love of each other, it was tribute to my sick father. I was aroused by the thought of doing such as I would not think it tribute, I would think it a sick play act showing what a sick fuck he was. My only concern was if my father would consider it a form of love in any manner.

"Candle burner, I think that my name for you is most right. You have been a light in that sick Ritual story. I will call my father and ask him if we are forbidden the Ritual."

Not waiting, I Willed my father to me. He stood to the side of us, offering a smile most pleasant.

"Yes. I expect tribute from you both. You have no love for each other. I will not take you for honoring me. It is good that you asked, for I can be fickle. So, let us be beyond such worry. Here, now, perform the Ritual. Elsa, as you cum, look into my eyes alone. Begin."

With that, a small vial of oil appeared in my hand. We were both naked, and my father was lounging on a cushion, waiting.

It took no thought, for the Ritual was inside us and was natural. Soon, we were covered in the oil, the serpent came out and entered me and it felt wonderful as it pushed through me, its head poking out of my mouth. As I was raised into the air, I fell back and hung with nothing but the feeling of being full inside where I had been empty. Moved to be where we could kiss, suddenly we were ablaze, and the fire was the first warmth I had felt since created. As the serpent released me, I fell onto cushions writhing in pleasure and gasping for I had never felt anything such. Scorpio remained standing, looking at my father for he worried that it was a deception, but it was not. My father looked to him, then to me.

"There, Elsa. Isn't that nice? At long last you are truly as your father. Fucked."

Scroll X
The Sweetness

Know that being starved, one will eat too much once finding food.
Having no love since made, with Scorpio I was hungry for what I
thought was loving embrace yet knew I could not love or be loved.
Yet Scorpio and I were both hungry and needed what we had found
in the Ritual. We were both in Thebes where I was watching over a
prize contract of my father's, Nefertiti. She was a foolish girl who sold
her soul and became more perverted than any man. Such a sick soul
was prized by my father and I endured her contract for a hundred
years. It was a time when I was isolated. With my time I scribbled
many scrolls on the nature of existence, evil, and humans.

When the day arrived when my father came to take his due with
the girl, I was free until his next prize contract was found. On my
own I was able to meet with Scorpio for the Ritual. In a secret
passage under the palace of the pharaohs, we met and after the
performing Ritual we relaxed and talked of our times and things
we longed for. I longed for one thing only, love, and told Scorpio
it was all I wished. I was naked as he could see all of me for he was
demon, even though a first Angel who had fallen, and could see
me that way. As I spoke of love I noticed he grew aroused. Know
it was not the serpent that rose from him, it was his human cock. I
thought only I was exciting him as a man, not a demon.

There, in the dark chamber, we had sex as humans and Angels
may do. It was like nothing I had ever known and was what I had
craved. Thinking nothing of my father, Scorpio being a first fallen
Angel, his first harvester, I thought it only his excitement as part
of the Ritual that we had never reached. He delighted in seeing me
in such passion and made him feel more than a harvester. It made
him feel as if an Angel in Heaven once more.

We went to his den of candles and there he sought no women to
harvest and laid with me. In his embrace I felt loved. As I reached

out for more loving, Scorpio mounted me from above. At that instant I felt the darkness of my father. He was there. The room turned black and my father was filled with ire watching us show what I thought to be love. He raised his hand and Scorpio rose off me into the air, unable to move. With his hand my father moved Scorpio to where his cock was above my face. I could not move except for my head. I looked at my father as his hand became a scythe and he cut Scorpios cock off. It landed on my face as Scorpio's body fell onto mine.

I looked to scream at my father, but he was gone. He had come to remind me that I could have love with none but him. Scorpio could perform the Ritual as it was not love, but he could not make love to me.

Scorpio's human form, the one he possessed while harvester, was bleeding and he was in agony. I went to a torch that lit the room and used it to cauterize the wound, hearing him scream. It stopped the bleeding. He would survive but he was in pain. Telling him I would go to the market for opium to stop the pain, I covered myself in my black burka and ran to the stalls and tents, looking for opium or anything that could help his pain. Searching, asking, pleading, none was to be found.

As I ran, I was drawn to an alley that housed no sellers. It was empty and full of dust. I could do nothing but stand there. I thought at first it was a call from my father, a way to tell me what wrong I had done, but it was not that at all. I watched as dust swirled around me, and I knew time had stopped. All of the market and sounds had vanished. It was only me standing in the alley watching dust spiral up and away. From the sky came a cloud and I felt elated looking up to it. It swirled in ways and colors that were beautiful and filled me with wonder. As the cloud reached to just above me, I saw a form within it, and it was an Angel of Heaven more beautiful than anything could be in all of existence. I had never seen a pure Angel of Heaven, and I realized that was what my father had once been. I could only wonder how he could turn away from being such.

 Lucifer's Daughter

Being hasataan, I had never known the Divine. It is not what one can think of or imagine. Divinity is so powerful it is all that exists when in its presence. There is no way to think of anything else, no way to feel anything other than its nature, and it is overwhelming. I was no longer Elsa, I was no longer hasataan, I was only one being Graced with the Holy Spirit of Divinity which is the love of the Father.

Created to be beauty, attraction, lust, and all any would die for, the presence of the Angel made me nothing more than a grain of sand, the same as I saw humans. I was nothing in the presence of Grace. All that I thought I was left me, and all I knew was the Angel descending from the sky above. Nothing else mattered, nothing else existed. At that moment, I knew nothing more. I only knew the love of the Father and the beauty of His creation. I thought of it all much later, as at that moment, I had no ability to think of myself.

As the cloud filled the alley it parted and I saw the Angel.

She was real not real. She was there not there. She was an ideal, not a reality. Nothing could be what she was. Even now I think of how I was unprepared for such wonder. To see something that was all there was, but only for me at that moment. I wanted to fall to my knees and give thanks for being gifted with her presence but could not do so. I knew she wished no worship or thanks. She was not a deity. She was not God. She was a spirit with form, not one to pray to.

With all the clouds parting I saw her fully. I understood the meaning of majestic for the first time, for she was that. I thought of all the fools who had sold their souls for beauty in a deal with my father, and he knew what real beauty was for he was once an Angel and knew the beauty of the Angelic. He never gave any human beauty. He gave them nothing.

Her form was both a thing that was seen and felt. The feeling was more beautiful than her form, yet her form was more beautiful than the feeling. They were one and the same, yet each was neither.

She was what I thought her to be at any moment.

As she floated above me, she looked at me and I rose in the air and was lifted to be at eye level with her. She was made of pure light, and she was transparent yet solid at the same time. She was tall, naked, surrounded by a sheer gossamer that circled her form, yet never touched it. She held one leg slightly higher than the other, and her legs were long and perfect, as was her entire form. Her breasts were the notion of what breasts must be, and her face was also an ideal. If anyone were to think of what a beautiful face was, hers would be what they would see. Again I knew her face was the nature of what a face was meant to be, and it was an ideal. Her hair was blonde, not golden, not one color. It was endless shades of blonde as if the Sun was shining on her hair from endless positions. Each strand was perfect, yet each strand was different. Her hair was long, and it was flowing in patterns around her head that never stayed the same as they formed perfect designs that made her more and more beautiful as I watched the patterns change.

Being lifted to gaze into her eyes, they were light blue, and like her hair the blue never stayed the same color of blue. They were infinite ideas of what blue must be. I could only marvel at all she was for she was ever changing, and being ever changing, that was what she looked like. Like a lush tree in the wind, it has a trunk, branches, and leaves. As you watch it remains a tree yet never remains the same. The shifting light of the day, the wind blowing, the branches bending… it is impossible to take one look at the tree then look again and say it looked the same. Yet, you know it is a tree. That was what the Angel was. Ever changing, ever the same, and it was in being ever changing that she looked the way she did. I know only she was the idea of what beautiful must be. I could no longer think myself beautiful as I had seen her, and I was in awe of her form.

As she looked at me, I was floating, and she let me know, not with words, but with her mind, that I was taken with her presence. I thought to her and said that was most true and that I had no idea of what the Grace of the Father was until seeing her. She thought to me that I was beautiful as her, for there was no other such as me. I was wonder to her as she was wonder to me. I thought that was impossible, and she said she understood. She said for her I was wondrous, and my spirit was so stunning she wished to show me how she saw me through the eyes of the Father.

She tilted her head down, looked at my burka, then closed her eyes seeing me with her spirit. When her eyes opened my black burka had vanished and I was wearing a white burka made of silk not of Earth, but of Heaven. I felt myself fully new and it was wonderful. I looked down and I saw that like her, I was majestic, for the white silk was an echo of the pure love inside of me. I was not Angel and I was not hasataan. I was Elsa. There was no other like me and she saw that. As I changed from being seen in her mind I became the true me I was since made. I thanked her. As we looked at each other I knew she thought of me only as who I was and not what my father wanted me to be.

Holding out her hand, she offered a small package wrapped in brown parchment and tied with brown cotton string. I took it, and to my mind she said it would heal pain as that was what I sought. I thanked her. As I put it in the pocket of my burka, all changed.

In less than an instant, the Angel had a blade of might in her hands and the blade was just as the one Michael held at the arch at the entry to Heaven. I felt it's power and I was lost in fear of it though Knowing it was not intended for me. The Blade was pure light and it reached to the sky and as I watched it, I knew it to be the power of Grace. The power of the Father. If one was not Graced, only then would it be feared.

I heard her voice for the first time. It was not a trumpet, it did not fill the skies or Heavens. It was quiet and determined and it was somber.

"I will strike, Uncle."

Looking down to the ground, I instantly looked to where her attention was. There, beneath us was my father. I knew then as she called him Uncle that she was more than an Angel of Heaven, she was the highest of all Angels. She was Gloria.

At that moment I understood that my father was both insane and ingenious. He had let me feel love for Scorpio, let him make love to me so he may castrate his human form and knew I would be seeking a remedy for pain. He had taken all opium from the market. He had longed for a way to call Gloria to his presence and had used my goodness and need to have her help me. He knew she would come as like her I was a victim of his perversion. I learned that we were alike in that way, and it was why she had appeared.

I worried not as she held the Blade that could cast him to nothingness. I had been told of the Blade by my father. If it heard a lie, if it heard intent to harm an Angel, if it was aware of any wrong to be done it would strike. If my father told the truth and offered no threat the Blade would remain at the ready but would not strike him down. My father, being Knowing, showed no fear of the Blade as he planned no lies and no harm.

"Gloria, my Sweetness, the Blade will not strike for I am here only to marvel at you. I have not seen you since the fall, and I have longed to see what a beautiful woman you have become. You have surpassed your mother in that way. I will let her know."

Humming, the Blade was not satisfied with what he said. As I remained high in the air, Gloria lowered herself to be just above my father, the Blade now laying above her shoulder and behind her back, ready to slice at my father's head.

"You will cross the line. Speaking of my mother is where the line exists as you have taken her from Heaven, my father, and me. Will you speak of her again?"

Growing brighter, the Blade was humming loud, but my father showed no concern.

"If what I say is true, I worry nothing of the Blade. I will speak that she chose to fall. She used her Free Will. She could have stayed with you and your father, but she chose to be with me."

Raising the Blade, Gloria was getting ready to strike him down. He was playing a game with her. He shrugged and looked hurt. She spoke to him again in a dark tone.

"Why are you here? Your daughter did not call to you."

"That is why, Sweetness. A father worries for his daughter. Have I not that right? Elsa was shopping in the market, going along as on any day, and then time stopped, you appeared, lifted her from the ground and it worried me. I asked what was the Holiest of all Angels doing with my daughter? I wish to be sure she is safe from you."

It was clear that my father was taunting her, and his reason was a lie. He cared not for me, he wished only to see his Sweetness. The Blade knew it was a lie and it made a sound that was as stars colliding and she swung the Blade with a might never known on Earth. It met with nothing for my father had vanished as he said his last word. She could not strike what was not there.

Watching the Blade return to its handle, she put it behind her neck and hair. Lifting her right hand upward, she was a beam of light ascending to Heaven where she came from, and I slowly was lowered to the ground. Suddenly, the alley was full of blowing dust and I could hear the sounds of the market as time had returned.

I walked to a large boulder in the alley, sat on it, taking out the small package she had given me. I untied the string and put it in my pocket to keep. Inside the parchment was a small brown vial. I knew it would take Scorpio's pain away. I folded the paper and put it in my pocket with the string.

I had witnessed a confrontation between the ultimate good and the ultimate evil. I was sure Gloria would always prevail. I knew I had been used by my father to bring Gloria to Earth, and I was sad for that. I would be sure to not let that happen again. I would love none.

From that day I was even sadder for I vowed to keep Gloria
away from me. She was the only one who had shown me love or
understanding. She saw me inside. With the white burka she gifted
me with understanding that I was not the blackness of my father.
Of all I have known, that gave me something I never had.

Hope.

Scroll XI

My Purpose

Know it was from encountering Gloria that I learned who I was, and I was not what my father created me to be. He sought to make me to show all that he had the same ability to create life from his sheer Will just as the Creator did. Although he did not intend to make me one with Free Will, he was foolish as any that lives has Free Will and I am proof of that.

Although not made by the Creator, I have life. The Creator may not have known that all living things created would have Free Will, as the only one not made by the Father of all Creation I have a Will of my own. I can not speak to the nature of being for I am not one who creates life, but I am testimony that as a living being, Free Will is the nature of being such. I look at a grub worm and it makes choices and travels with one worm when there are many more around it. I look at myself and see that I have chosen to not be as my father. While many are imprisoned or controlled by another as a slave, they may not act and do what they wish, but that is only because of the threat to their being, not their Will.

In the desert I heard a wise man being followed tell those who listened that to find peace, one must accept everything. I felt ire hearing such a controlling message, but I judged too soon. He followed that to find peace one must accept things, but that does not mean you have to like them. He was asked was that not a contradiction, and his reply was wise. He said that to make a change, accepting the truth is the only way to fight it or change that truth.

There are not many humans who have purpose or Knowing, but the wise man opened my eyes with wisdom. Hearing his message, I understood to defy my father I must accept that he was the way he was. I could not change him, but I could change my view of him and know I was not his to control.

I could be that in mind and purpose yet I had his chain around my neck. That would keep me a prisoner if I fought it. I changed my Knowing that although chained to him I was a free woman. He could hold me but could not change my Will. He could keep me from one I love, but not keep me from loving in spirit. It was then I understood the wise man had shown me the path to free myself from my father. Only by accepting him could I change myself. The only one I could change was me.

I wrote a scroll on the matter and placed it in a hall of knowledge along with many other scrolls of philosophy. Know that my scroll has been used ever since by those seeking truth.

Filled with that Knowing I was the one holding myself prisoner, I let myself go. I was prepared for the time when my father ordered me to go to Heaven and have Michael, his brother the Archangel, fall in love with me.

He called me to his chambers hidden under abaddon. As I appeared he was looking over maps of Heaven he had drawn in preparation for my meeting Michael. Reclining on his divan I looked at all he made there. Divan, large table where he worked, chairs, frames, cabinets for his contracts… all were carved by his hand from the Tree of Life in the Garden when he was the serpent and defiled Eve. He prized his corruption of all humans and when the Garden was left to decay he took the tree he coiled in as serpent and it was a trophy in his sick mind. I saw he had made a new stand for large candles and I commented on it.

"Are you ever going to run out of wood from that fucking tree?"

Bringing maps to the divan, he put them on a wood table in front of it and sat on a wooden chair across from me.

"There is much left. Would you like a divan or table? I can carve one for you."

"Father, did you not gather that I was mocking your obsession with that fucking tree?"

Smiling at me, he shrugged and acted as if hurt.

"Daughter, I know you have yet to do such a momentous thing, so do not understand. The wood is not about the tree or the Garden. It's about fucking Eve. Taking away her faith in the Father and defiling his first humans. When I look at wood here, I think of how I fucked that cunt to where no human cock would satisfy a human woman ever again. Giving her my serpent, knowing what a real fuck was, there would never be a time when a human woman would be happy with a human man. Only a demon with a serpent."

Having heard the story before it was a chance to remind him what a fool he was.

"And how was Eve? Was she worth all that trouble?"

"Oh, Eve? No! She was a lousy fuck! Pretty, I guess. No. It was the thrill of taking away what my Father created her to be. Pure. Good. Devoted to Him. But he really fucked up with Free Will and she used her fucking Free Will alright. She used it on my serpent for a month without stopping. All that no-dick Adam could do was watch and cry. You should have seen him… Begging the Father to stop her. The Fucker can't stop anyone. She made her choice. Serpent. Me."

"Was it really a choice? Or did you lie and deceive her that showing her Free Will to take the fruit of the tree, your fucking serpent, was a way to thank your Father for giving her a choice?"

"Of course I did."

"Father, cunt like that is only something to be proud of if she wanted you. Loved you. Deceived such, you could have done as much if you fucked the knot hole in the tree as she had no love for you. I think it's your saddest take ever. Pathetic."

Still smiling, he told me I was yet to learn, but I was about to.

"How can I learn to be fucking pathetic? I'm not."

"Being pathetic may be good for you. You wish to be loved. To have that you must surrender yourself to another and that is truly pathetic."

"Father, stop and think of what you said. You have ruined your existence for the Angel girl. You want her to love you. Do you mean you will surrender yourself to her?"

Filling his chambers with laughter, he couldn't talk as he was in hysterics. He calmed down after some time then looked at me with a somber look.

"You are being defiant to rile me, correct? I hope so, or I'll have to shoot some seed across existence and make a new daughter. Stop thinking with your cunt. It's to have her surrender to me."

It is true I knew that, and all I said was to rile him.

"You have only spoke true one time. That I am defiant to rile you. I will never be anything other than defiant of you just as you are defiant of your Father."

"That is what I expect of you, of course. I meant that you didn't know I would not surrender to any. That she must surrender to me. I spoke true."

"You spoke a fantasy, not true. She will never surrender to you. She is not dumb fuck Eve who fell for your game. That will never happen, so that is why you did not speak true."

"Elsa, that is a good point. As things are now, you speak true. Your father has plans to change that and that is why I summoned you. You will be what makes my Sweetness beg to surrender to me. Seriously, Elsa. Give me at least that much respect. I have defiled all things. She is the last to conquer. The Sweetness will be mine."

Watching him, he was fully sincere. I sought to taunt him, but with the wisdom of accepting things to change them, I was accepting that he had a plan and I was part of it. I asked how.

"There, there. Finally, a true hasataan. There is no need to be a brat. I made it where you met my Sweetness. What did you think of her?"

"What I thought is what I think. You will never be deserving of her and she will never relent."

"Did you think her beautiful?"

"She is beyond beauty. You know that."

"I do. Wait until you meet my brother. Michael is the same. He is beyond all men just as she is beyond all women. Michael… well… I am not certain how to say it but he shall be your Sweetness. Once you look into his eyes you will be as me with Gloria. I speak true."

There are few times my father has ever spoke true. The first was when he told me he suffered the loss of being loved by the Father. This time he also revealed to me what none other would ever know.

"These maps are the way into Heaven. It will lead you where Michael loves to meditate. An apple grove. Ah, yes, in the trees just like Eve in the Garden. You will go there and you will meet your Sweetness. You will love him and he will love you. I made you to be the only one he can love as he did Ethereal. I know what he loved about her, for I ate her soul. That attraction you have is the attraction of Ethereal. He will be yours in an instant. One look from your eyes. And as he is the one who can strike me to nothingness, he will be the one you love. He is the one who is not afraid of me in any way. Being the most beautiful as a First Angel, and wanting to free you from your chain, your love will be beyond all loves. He is your Savior."

My whole being was shaken. All he said was true. It was then I accepted he knew what he was doing when he took Ethereal on the day of the fall. It was for this day. It was to create me with her inside of me. From the day he fell and made abaddon when Michael went to save Ethereal, as an eternal being he waited long to make his revenge the most painful it could be. I was part of it.

"You have commanded that I love none but you. You have said you will never hurt me but will destroy any who loves me or any I love. Yet you are saying I will love Michael and he will love me. Since that cannot be will you destroy him?"

"Daughter, please, you are full hasataan and can see what is to be. Do so."

As I stared at the map, I thought of all that he said and realized how ingenious his plan was.

"The chain... It is why I wear the chain... I can enter Heaven, you cannot. When I am in Michael's embrace you will pull me from him. You cannot harm him or take him but you can take me away from him and hurt him once more."

"A good start. I love hurting Michael but that is not what gets my Sweetness to me. To surrender to me. Think more... When Michael loses your cunt and is ready to fall to follow you, what will happen?"

As I did, I was enraged.

"Michael lost his love and wife, and Gloria has seen and lived with the guilt of that. She will not wish him to ever suffer more. I see it all now. Seeing Michael happy with my love and then you pulling me from him… To return me to him you will offer her a deal…"

"Ah, as if I thought of it myself. Good. That is right. Gloria will have no choice but to surrender herself to me if I take your chain away and let you return to her father. He would have you, I would have my Sweetness. Cunt for cunt. That, daughter, is a fair deal."

"Father, you are using me to harm Gloria. I will not do that."

"No. You won't. Gloria will make her own decision. It is her choice. Her father, or herself."

There was a look in his eyes that let me know there was more than what he had told. I said nothing for he would not reveal more. He was counting on my need for love to be like him. Without regard for who was hurt. He thought Gloria giving herself in my stead would mean nothing to me. He was hiding that he knew I would do everything to have love, save Gloria and Michael, and harm him. He wouldn't send me if he didn't have a deeper plan to deal with my defiance. As I looked at him, he knew I was aware of that.

"Yes. You are Knowing. I will not let you change the outcome. I have described the simple way to do what was said. If needed I will do more. I assure you that I will have my Sweetness."

I was with eyes closed, and I saw true.

"But I will not have Michael."

The look in his eyes was one I shall never forget. He nodded, and this time there was no smile.

"That is so. When I have my Sweetness, I will fuck her endlessly and will not be here running this pit. You will run it. Having lost the love of Michael will make you the true hasataan. Not a First Angel, not of the Father, filled with pain because the Father made

Free Will and let all this horror happen, you will be what I have
been. A demon filled with pain. The loss of love. And you will hate
not only the Father, you will hate me as never before."

I stood up, took the maps, and looked at him.

"You are right. I am hasataan. Just as you, I will fall from your
grace although that is not what it is. Your Father didn't expect you
to fall or create suffering. He expected you to do what He wished.
As my maker, you are doing the same. You expect me to do what
you wish. But we hasataans, we are not ones to do what their
maker expects them to do…"

With that, I willed myself to the waterfall where he fell from Grace
to the black nothing of infinity. His way out was my way in. He
had made one mistake. He forgot I had my own Will, not his.

Folio III
Scroll XII

Scroll XII

My Garden

Know when I went to Heaven, it was not what I expected and not what I had ever known. My first thought was of how my father could have wished to leave. It was a place to ascend to, not fall from. There were no palaces, no fools walking about in finery. It was filled with fields and forests, trees and groves, rivers and lakes, and it had a feeling of peace. Peace is not something one such as I knew until then. As I walked down a simple path I felt safe. I had no need to cover my face or body although I would go nowhere without the silk Gloria had graced me with and it was what I was wearing.

Beyond wonder of the lack of anything to impress anyone there, as I looked to the sky it was ever changing. At first I thought that was the nature of the sky there but that was not so. If I thought of blue it was blue. If I thought of clouds it was filled with clouds. If I thought of my sadness it responded with birds circling me and singing a song that took my sadness from me. All of Heaven was such. It was ever changing to make me feel wanted, at peace, and amazed. I could never have imagined it being such for one cannot imagine a place that was the meaning of imagination and wonder. How could I have seen such skies or rivers where all the fish swam up to greet me, where chipmunks knew where I wished to go and scampered ahead to show the way?

Walking, thinking of meeting Michael, the wind was blowing and it sang a song to me of love although it had no words I understood. I let go of the maps and they flew up to the sky and became ravens that turned back from where I came and I watched as they flew, large and solemn, past the waterfall then sailed straight down to where abaddon lay. The chipmunks knew where I was headed and I was free from my father except for the vile chain of a serpent that circled my neck. Even with it there, the only reminder was that I was going to stop him from his plan.

Soon, the chipmunks ran to a grove of trees and burrowed in the ground as they knew it was a place for Michael and me alone. I used thoughts to thank them and stood in the shade of the trees in the grove. I knew it was not like the Garden in any manner. It was a simple grove of apple trees, and it was a place to rest and contemplate existence if one wished. As I looked up at the apples I saw they were all perfect and ripe. Just seeing them made me realize I was hungry for I had travelled far and they looked wonderful as I ate no animal flesh.

I reached up to one branch, then another. Know that I am a little thing. I am small in every way, and slight in form. As I reached to the lowest branch I could find, I was on the tips of my toes, with both of my arms reaching high as I could make them go but they were still not high enough to reach an apple.

Frustrated by my lack of height, it is true that I could float up but wished no demon power in that place. Thinking ripe apples would fall when ready, I went to the trunk of a tree that was the smallest in size and taking both my hands shook it with all my might, which I will say is not much for I am not made for shaking a tree. Looking up, I shook my head as all the apples held tight to their branches and I called out do they not wish to help one so hungry? The wind moved them as I wished the wind to blow, just gently, and even the wind did not shake the apples. Not even one dropped from the movement given them by the wind.

I saw one branch that seemed to hang lower and again I got on my toes and used both hands to reach for the nearest apple. It was beyond my grasp but I kept trying.

As I looked above to the branch I saw a sight I will always cherish. A gentle hand reached far above mine and took the finest apple from the tree and handed it to me.

I turned and there was Michael. He was beyond what I could imagine. He was a man. Just a man like one may see in a good place doing some kind thing. That was his form and he was handsome as Gloria was beautiful although that meant nothing compared to his spirit. The way he looked at me. The gentle smile. The way the wind I had asked to blow sent his hair behind his head so I could see all his face. I found that we were both holding the apple. As I took it, he was looking at me and hadn't let go of it. Our eyes looked only at each other, and it was a look I had longed to see since made. A look of love. Not what love could be, what love was. I wished to let him know I was thankful for his help.

"Thank you. I have been hungry for a long time."

After I said that, I took a large bite from the apple. I have had fruit of all varieties but none could ever be like that apple. It filled me with all I needed. It was if the apple was what I was inside. I looked at where I had bit and saw my teeth like a carving in the fruit. Eating it, not yet swallowing it all, I handed it up to Michael to share its wonder with him. As I held it he bent over and took a large bite. He closed his eyes as he chewed looking Joyous. Looking at the apple, I saw the small bite from my mouth and the large bite from his. Lifting it, when his eyes opened he looked at it and saw what I did. The two bites formed a symbol that meant two joined as one.

Taking my hand, he sat down beneath the tree and his hand did not pull, it welcomed me to sit with him.

There are moments that are remembered for they change all things you know. I have never known a moment like the one when I sat on the ground under the tree with Michael. I looked at him, then all around me, and I smiled as I talked softly to him.

"This is where I have longed to be. I have never known this. It is wonder beyond wonder when you gave the apple to me and looked into my eyes."

His eyes answered and told me stories I had existed to hear. They drew me into him, a place I wanted to be. They were welcoming me, accepting me, praising me, and they were loving me. I looked at him and hoped he could see the same in my eyes. He gently spoke.

"I see, and I have no words that can express my Joy. Hello."

Smiling, my face free to be seen, my smile there to give, I said hello back. It was as if I had filled him with comfort and Joy. I could see my hello wash over him, fill him, absorb into him. All that I am flowed into him just as he had entered me with but a look.

"Michael, I have come to find you. I will hide nothing as I want only you to know me true. I am Elsa, and I am the daughter of your sick brother…"

With the softest smile I had ever seen, he nodded slightly, and said he knew.

"We all come from someplace. Where we are from does not tell us where we will go. I felt you when you came here. I felt a goodness… a longing… and I felt love calling to me. It is why I am here with you. That was you I felt. It is something I once had but lost. I've longed to feel it again for time long."

All his words were as music. They were a symphony of words not words. Each word was like a drop of rain falling on me, each one soaking into me. I had no words. I had spoke true. I was Elsa, and that was all I needed to say. I found that each move I made was not one I decided on. I was being moved by Heaven, the sky, the wind, the apple, and the look in Michael's eyes.

I tugged at his sleeve to have him bend down to where I could be in front of his face and I kissed him.

It was my first true kiss. It was more than physical. It was pure spirit and it was welcomed and he kissed me back while taking his arms and wrapping them around me. I was being kissed, hugged,

understood, accepted, wanted, embraced. It was as natural as all of
Heaven to want to be with him, be one with him, give him love
in every way. I had not thought of the foolish sex of humans but
without thinking of it, I pulled off my white silk his daughter had
given me and let it fall beside us. We both lay under the branch
where he took an apple for me and looked into each other's eyes. I
raised myself high on my knees and leaning over, kissed him with
a passion that had been hidden in me since made. The kiss was all
of me flowing into him. My tongue, my spit, my moans, my body
rubbing against him all sang my song of love. It was me giving my
self, my entire being, to him.

It was answered by him and he had the same passion to give
himself to me. Kneeling up, him between both of my legs, I felt
his cock between them for it had grown large and hard and I knew
that was him giving himself, reaching to me. It was all of him and
he was longing to be in me as I was in him. I lowered myself onto
him and he filled me with his shaft. Like his kiss, it gave all he was
to me at the same instant. We were in Union, a place I had never
been. My head looked down, my eyes into his, large, stunned,
tears pouring from them. He looked at me and nodded to let all of
him flow into me.

I sat straight up, following to where his cock pointed, and put
both my arms straight up into the air as I gyrated on him so
he could see all of me, and I knew I was a wonder to see. Every
muscle, every part of me was rippling as I moved up and down
on him. The feeling was so powerful, so intense, that all I was went
into a spasm. My body was shaking, my head rolling, my long
brown hair flying in every direction, and both in form and spirit
I was no longer me. I didn't know who or what I was. All I knew
was that he was in me, with me, for me, carrying me to the place
where Angels dwell for I was truly in Heaven beyond Heaven at
that moment.

Seeing me have my first climax, he was doing the same although
not his first. His body was in spasms, his hands rubbing me in

all places, and I found his finger in my mouth and I sucked on it as if his finger was my life, my existence, and I would be nothing without it. As I sucked hard as I could on his finger, I felt him erupt inside of me. Like a waterfall flowing up, he filled me with his very being. I stopped moving, just looked into his eyes, feeling each pulse inside of me. I wanted his stream to never stop filling me. It was his love. It was all I would ever want or need.

Watching my reaction, he closed his eyes and let the moment be in his mind for he was seeing my spirit, and wanted only to feel how I took his stream and how it filled me, became part of me, making me Holy for I was filled with the Angel of God and I was his alone and knew he was mine.

As I shouted out thanks to the Father for his son, we heard something neither expected.

"Daddy!"

Scroll XIII

Blessing

Know only I saw the look of understanding on his face. I turned and there was Gloria, hands on her hips, a look of shock on her face, her long blonde hair flying behind her. She was so tall, so majestic, and her eyes were wide with disbelief. She was looking at both of us, then looked all around and I knew she worried my father was there, hiding, but she quickly stopped looking for that could never be. Michael sat up, holding me, and I lifted off him to sit by his side as I looked up at Gloria, my face showing a look of hoping she would understand and be Joyous for our love.

"Gloria, I can see you are surprised…"

"Surprised? Surprised! That doesn't describe what I am. What are you doing?"

"This is Elsa…"

Before he could say more, she reacted in disbelief.

"I know who she is. I went to her on Earth, remember? When uncle tried to take me!"

"Gloria, I saw her reaching for an apple. She was hungry. I offered her comfort."

"Comfort? Is that what it's called now? Oh, I'll go tell all to give comfort to any they wish. This place will be wilder than when we went to Sodom!"

"She is so small… She was reaching up far as she could and I picked an apple for her."

"Oh… Oh! This is her thanks for getting an apple for her? And Elsa. Using that trick! Reaching way up, those little breasts

pointing up, your perfect bottom out, back arched, and my silk, transparent and letting him see all of you that way? You sunk to that? Oh! Look at my silk! That is your thanks for such a blessing?"

I could only speak true.

"Gloria, I treasure it."

"Really, you treasure it? And there it is, laying in the dirt. Cast off while you had your way with my daddy!"

She was right. In my passion I had let it fall to my side on the ground. I reached for it and brushed it off, making sure it was perfect, then sitting with my knees up to my chin I folded it and put it between my legs and breasts.

"I do."

Michael reached and put his arm around me, pulling me to him, smiling at his daughter as he understood her reaction.

"Gloria, it was unexpected and I wish to share our happiness with you. Please, sit with us."

Shaking her head, Gloria let out a sigh, knelt in front of us, then lowered herself to sit on her hip, her arm supporting her to look right at us.

"Gloria, if it were not unexpected, I would have told you in a different way."

"Unexpected? Father. Unexpected is going to walk in the flowers with Father and learning he had a new rose that was His Vision of me. That was unexpected. I came to tell you of it, and did I find my father waiting to hear? No, he's on the ground doing Luce's daughter like he's never had a wife to cherish. Oh, even worse.

Like he's never had a hot number before. My mother was the most beautiful of all in creation…"

Seeing the look on her face, I understood. She took his loving me as a betrayal of her mother. My father had taken her mother's existence. How could she feel other? It was not my place to speak, and I knew Michael understood more than I what Gloria was feeling.

"Gloria. I understand. I'm sorry I hurt you. Know this. I speak true. Your mother is gone. My love for her is as yours. Eternal and true. You know that. Do you see other in me right now?"

Gloria looked at him for a long time, then closed her eyes and touched his leg. As she opened her eyes, she shook her head.

"Nothing other. Your love for her is stronger than ever before this day. I am sorry for saying hurtful things to you. I am young and foolish and I reacted before Knowing."

"Gloria, I understand. I have longed for you to have a love. You know that. I know that if you do, my brother will use any you love to take you. It is why I drew the line. You know that is true."

Nodding, Gloria was crying. She didn't need to say anything. He was her father and he had lived only for her since the fall. He continued to speak to her of his feelings.

"I have been alone a long time. Not from choice. I had never known any I could feel love for the way a mate must be loved. When I saw Elsa, all that appeared. I felt love that is true. There is no doubt in me, and she offered no temptation."

Gloria was surprised at all he said. I knew why but could not say. She looked to me and grew serious.

"Elsa. Speak true. Are you not the meaning of temptation? Lust?

Desire? Can any resist you with those big eyes of yours batting at them? How could you not tempt him?"

I was indeed looking up at her with my big eyes as I said much with them, not words. And it was true they were batting at her. I could only speak true.

"You are right. Lucifer made me to be those things. But only to ones not Holy, ones who will sin. I did none of that with Michael. I did not go to him. I am filled with Joy for he came to me."

Looking at me, thinking, I could see she had concerns. She spoke them.

"Elsa. Speak true when I ask you what I must."

"Gloria. I cannot lie. I can only speak true."

"Then, why are you here? How did you enter where no demon may go?"

"Gloria, nothing stopped me from entering for I am no fallen Angel, and I am no demon. I am Elsa, nothing else. I am the only one of my kind. I was welcomed into Heaven and I did nothing but walk in. I said that first to answer your first question with Knowing. I was sent here, by my father, to find Michael and make him fall in love with me."

Staring at me, Gloria's eyes widened and she looked only to me, not Michael.

"Know this. If you lie or deceive, the Blade my father and I wield will blaze and strike and you will be no more…"

"That is not a worry for me, Gloria. I told you I can only speak true. I have."

Eyes squinting, Gloria reminded herself that if I said anything but the truth that both their Blades would strike me to nothingness. She nodded, sure of matters, then continued.

"My uncle commanded you here to take my father's heart. Once you have it, which it seems you do already, what are you to do with it?"

"My father bids me to break his heart, and then leave him alone without my love."

Gasping, Gloria looked at me and she didn't need her Blade. Her look was a Blade every bit as strong. She sat, looking to Michael and me, wanting an explanation.

"There is more. Gloria, it is not only to hurt Michael. My father said that would be a delight, but it is not why I am here. The reason will strike ire in you, as it does in me. I will tell of it, but it will upset all of us. I wish to just say it, and we can talk of it after if you will give me that gift."

Taking a deep breath, she braced herself. I saw how amazingly beautiful Gloria was. Angry, filled with wrath, she was more stunning than when not. I saw her nod, then looked to Michael and kissed his hand holding mine.

"Gloria… My father is mad, but still more insidious and genius than can be imagined. He wishes me to leave your father so devastated that you will hurt seeing him so. To take care of your father, he knows you will follow me to bring me back. When that happens, he will be waiting to take you. He calls you only his Sweetness and is sure you are his. His possession. It is all about having you. He created me to be as wondrous as you for this very day. I am sorry with all I am."

Neither Gloria nor Michael looked at me with any animus. Both knew what I told was of my father's design, never mine. After looking at each other, Michael looked to me and I saw a sadness

  Lucifer's Daughter

in his look that was as deep as his look of love for me. He was a
Supreme being with far more Knowing than my father and knew
what that meant for each of us. He reached and rubbed Gloria's
cheek, sad that she again was being hurt and feeling shame for
being what my father craved. Her face fell into his hand, and it
was a sight I will always treasure. A father holding and giving
understanding to his daughter. I had never had such kindness or
love. If one deserved such, it was Gloria. I would do anything for
her for she has suffered more than me although she thinks it is I
who has endured the most.

Looking at me, she was crying for me, not herself. Michael
understood.

"Elsa, my brother has done such harm to us, and Ethereal. Now,
he is doing even worse to you. In his plan, he leaves you without
my love. He thinks only of his madness for my daughter. Gloria is
a warrior. She will extinguish his flame. It grows to consume us all
and it must be stopped. You were made to be loved, and now that
you found love he will take it from you. That cannot be. I let that
happen to Ethereal. I will not let that happen to you."

Rising up, standing tall and mighty, I watched as Wings appeared
behind Gloria. Like all the mysteries of Heaven they were beyond
all that could possibly be. They grew as large as the sky above
us. They were not made of feathers for they were made of light.
As they moved, she raised just slightly above the ground. Just as
when seeing her for the first time, she held one leg slightly up, and
her right hand was up, one finger up in proclamation. Her gossamer
sheath had changed to a crystal armor that was both frightening and
beautiful to behold. I was looking at the true Guardian.

"Father, this ends now. I must go talk to Father. I will no longer
allow my uncle to do his bidding."

With that, her Wings flapped and all the trees behind us bent
from the might of the wind from them, all their apples falling to

the ground. I watched as she ascended and she looked down to us, nodding, letting us know she would stop my father. Turning, she flew away, sending ripples through every field in Heaven, her wrath plain to see as the lights of her Wings grew bright red and became flames.

Scroll XIV

Visitor

Know that after Gloria left, Michael said that as the Guardian, we would be safe for my father could not enter Heaven, and he knew that I did not intend to do what my father expected of me. He put his finger under my chin as I looked up at him. I rarely speak and find that my eyes say more than my words, and he understood my true language was the look on my face. He kept his finger under my chin as he stood up, leaning over me still, then moved his hand to take mine.

"A battle has been raging since the fall. I once thought it was my battle to avenge what my brother did to Ethereal. It changed to protecting Gloria from him, but protecting is not the same as stopping him. Gloria has come to understand that stopping your father is the only peace all in Creation will know. The ultimate battle is not between me and my brother, it is between Gloria and him. I am Knowing she no longer will wait for him to cross the line. She will draw a new one and it is one he will have to cross. When he does, he will be cast to nothingness. So, worry not. I want to hold you. To be inside of you. I wish only to fill you with the love you have opened up in me. Come with me."

There was no need for an answer. I stood, his hand pulling me up. I watched as he put on his sheath, and he watched as I put on my silk. Once dressed, I tugged at the arm of his sheath, and he leaned down to listen. I answered with a kiss long and loving.

It was a beautiful day and we walked to his hovel. The First Angel had no palace. He and Gloria lived in a simple hut made from mud and wood he had crafted by hand. Inside there was a room for him, a smaller room for Gloria, and a room where one entered with a table and chairs and a simple stove for cooking. Outside was a pond and a creek feeding it where they took water, and it

was surrounded by white trees with bright green leaves. It was a place of comfort and was filled with love.

Michael kept holding my hand as I stopped to look at things. A basket filled with memories. A ribbon, a letter, a brush for hair. There was a book full of drawings made by Gloria when she was little, and some included my father before the fall, and she was smiling in them and it upset me as she had drawn my father smiling at her even more, and I know she had drawn true. There wasn't much there, but each thing was for purpose or a memory. On the table was a variety of fruits, and a jug for water from the creek.

I looked up and batted my eyes to let Michael know I had looked at all the things, and he led me to his room. It had a soft bed, candles, and one cabinet and a small window. It was covered in a tapestry of a forest of Evergreen trees, and after I looked around, I tugged at his sleeve. He smiled knowing what I wanted and took it off as I took off my silk. I folded both and put them on the cabinet with care, and he pulled the sheets down and was laying in the bed waiting for me. I stood and looked at him grow hard, and I went and kissed his cock then began taking it in my mouth. I moved my head up and down, and as I did so I moved to where my holes were above his mouth and he was kissing them tenderly and probing them with his tongue. I was trembling with passion and everything I did was loving and felt right to do. Again we were joined as one. I had him in me, he was inside of me. The flow of our love moved in a circle between our mouths and I felt it go from where he licked to where I sucked and it circled round and round. I loved each move, each lick, each sound, and I could live holding each other such forever. I was filled with love of body and spirit. I was learning how form echoed spirit and why we have both.

As I took him all the way down my throat, there was a knock on the door frame to the room, and I moved only my eyes to see what was causing the knocking. It was the Father, watching us, waiting for a chance to gain our attention. Michael welcomed Him, and said he was longing to have us meet. I pulled Michael from my throat, crawled off the bed then went to Him and hugged Him with all my love and respect, and he put His head on mine, and patted my back as I hugged, crying, saying I wanted to thank Him for Michael and Gloria, and for letting me be in His home.

"Father, I know You know, but this is Elsa, and I love her."

I pulled away slightly to look up at Him, and He smiled at me.

"Oh, Elsa. The love in you is a power that will light the way for all who wish to love another. What a beautiful mystery you are. I have longed to know you. I am honored to meet you."

His words were a shock to me. In Heaven, I was understood. I was respected. The Creator held me as His own child. He was truly the Father. I felt it. I could only speak true and tell Him.

"May I be your child? I want so much for You to be my Father for I have none."

"Elsa, you are My child. I am your Father. Would you like to understand that has always been?"

I looked up at Him, eyes batting.

"Elsa, Michael, let us sit at the table. I have brought apricots and have much to tell."

Smiling, I reached for my silk, anxious for Him to see me with the Blessing Gloria had given me. As Michael put on his sheath, I held it out for Him to feel, saying it was given to me by Gloria and she had saved me. He rubbed it, and then took it and held it above me as I held my arms up, and He lowered it onto me, dressing me. I can't describe being dressed by God, but it touched me and made me understand Him as few could. I was a child being dressed by a loving parent.

Sitting at the table, He said He had much news, but first He wished to explain how I was his child.

"It is simple. I created Lucifer, and he is my child. When a child of mine has a child, they are also a child of mine. Lucifer has you thinking that you are his alone. How could that be? Without Me he would not exist. All he made you with came from Me. His power to make you is a power I gave to him. You are my child like all in Creation. I am the true Father. Your Father. I hope that can be understood after all the lies he told you."

I answered with my eyes, and I was elated. We smiled at each other, and He took my hand and squeezed it tight, and I felt a force flow from Him into me. It was the stuff of Angels, and He looked at me.

"That is what he denied you. Divinity. That is Grace. My love. You are no demon. You are an Angel of Heaven."

Again, I went and hugged Him, and my hugs and kisses made Him smile and He was Joyous. As we looked at each other, we both had an understanding and it has never ceased since then. As I sat, He began to shake His head.

"Ah, my children. Full of surprises and wonders. Michael, I had a visit from a somewhat determined young Angel girl a while ago. I think you may know her, but for a while I did not recognize her. She was like nothing I've known before. Her Wings were made of fire and she was filled with wrath. I almost hid under the porch!"

Michael was laughing, as was I for we knew He spoke of Gloria. Michael smiled, clearly proud of her. He asked how He found the courage to face her.

"She saw Me hiding behind the door, and let her Wings fly away and she went to Me and said it was time for us to talk and pulled at My robe. How could I say no? She's not one to mess with!"

Michael was laughing harder, saying he could see it all, then held his hand up and showed a Vision of what Gloria had done. She pulled at the Father to have Him sit on the porch at the table there, then she reached behind her hair and pulled out the handle of her Blade and let it drop to the table, making a loud thud. Michael was going to put the Vision away, but the Father said He would love seeing her doing it all again, so we all watched.

"I am Archangel no longer. I am going wayward. I treasure my father drawing the line in the sand to protect me, but I honor it no longer. That line protects only Angels in Heaven. It doesn't protect those hurt on Earth, and it doesn't protect Elsa. I am going to the waterfall and I'm going to fall from Heaven and cast my uncle to nothingness. I don't need him to lie or threaten me. That's no more. There is a new line. I'm drawing it. It's the line between good and evil, right and wrong. There. Take your Blade and your line and you can…"

The Vision froze at that point, and Michael looked shocked. He said he was afraid to hear what she was going to tell Him to do with them. Father laughed, saying whatever she said was what she needed to say.

Watching the Vision start, she told the Father He could take the Blade and the line and He could defend Heaven himself as there will be little to do as Lucifer was going to face his doom. Her.

"You can stand at the Arch and philosophize and ponder things. I'm off to abaddon. I don't have a Blade, and this one is useless. It only fires if I'm lied to or threatened. Father, don't you understand Luce knows that? He's a smart one and I think he's figured it all out."

Michael and I watched in awe. She was marvelous. She was everything I hoped to be, but wasn't. I knew I was what she longed to be but wasn't. I thought in the future we could teach each other much. In the Vision, Father shrugged His shoulders.

"Why not get one that strikes him down because you want his evil to stop hurting everyone?"

   Lucifer's Daughter

That gave Gloria pause. She stood there, looking at Him, confused.

"So, if I want a Blade that could strike him down for what he's done, not what he's doing, where is that going to come from?"

Reaching to a table on the porch, there was a wooden box. He handed it to Gloria.

"Maybe from here. From Me?"

Opening the box, she took out a handle of pure white, and as she gave it a serious look, it's Blade fired and it was appearing only because she commanded it to. It was more powerful than the first Blade, and she went and began cutting at trees and they vanished with each strike. She shut her eyes for a blink and the Blade went away and into the handle. Looking at it, and Him, she put the handle behind her neck where it vanished until she wanted it to appear.

"I am sorry for striking the trees."

"They will grow back. Gloria, Ethereal won't. You won't if Lucifer has his way. Is that what you wished for?"

"Father, yes! But why… Why wait until now?"

"I can't influence you or tell you what to do. You know that would be going against the Free Will of all in Creation, and yes, Lucifer too. I didn't stop him from falling. The first Blade was your father's Will. This one is yours. This is the first time you asked for this. If you ask, I can give."

"Father, you know sometimes I just want to fly off with You and drop you in abaddon and see what You would do there? I wonder how much of that Free Will stuff would stand when all hell is about to eat Your existence."

"Oh, I'd stop them. They'd all vanish. Gloria, figure it out. I have Free Will too. That would be my decision."

She stood, hands on hips.

"Your are hopeless and impossible. I mean, You could have given me a hint. A little nudge."

"And, Gloria, you could have asked Me for one…"

She stood, clearly flustered.

"It's like playing cards with You. I know You stack the deck and play Your cards close to Your sheath. I need to do battle, and not with Your card tricks. With the hasataan. So, if I still have Wings, and I am still Your Holiest Angel, I need to fly. Oh, Luce's daughter is here, and she's going at my dad nonstop so if you can pull them apart, can you please tell them I'm off to stop my uncle once and for all?"

Not waiting for an answer, her Wings were white light again and she filled the sky beyond Heaven with them, and just before flying away, she leaned over and gave the Father a sweet kiss.

Fading, Father was smiling.

"She is marvelous. Can she be any braver? I don't know… With the Blade she has, she has a lot to do. Luce and all his minions. Elsa, what did you think of all of that?"

Wanting to say that was incredible, I could only speak true.

"Gloria will do what she said, but it will not be easy. My father… he knows she will find a way to strike him down. I think he's prepared for that. I don't know what, but he sent me here to provoke her for a reason. And she is provoked which was his intent. I worry."

I watched as Father stood up, and He put His hands on our heads.

"Elsa, you know your father well. He hides in his madness. I have no worry for Gloria. She is invincible. He has never said he would get her by taking her. He has said she will surrender to him by hurting the ones she loves. I worry that. Be aware that you are both the ones she loves."

With that, He was gone.

Scroll XV
The Chain

Know that with Gloria having her new Blade, Michael and I knew my father still wished me to do what he commanded. I shared my father had given me no time when I must break Michael's heart. Michael confided that if Gloria was successful in locating him there would be no need for such a task as he would be no more. I knew that my arriving in Heaven, falling in love with Michael, had prompted Gloria to take Blade and find my father which was his true intent. Until Gloria returned I decided to put what my father wished aside and worry only of Michael and our love.

While waiting for Gloria we spent our time in constant embrace and passion. We were both without love for so long we were empty vessels needing to be filled. Only I could fill him. Only he could fill me.

With love given with form, it opened more ways to each other in spirit. I learned of Michael's most precious memories, heard the horrific way he watched my father go from First Angel to the hasataan and how his wife Ethereal had lost her existence to save little Gloria. Having always known my father to be insane, what astonished me was how that was all he was. Insane. Mad. Sick. All speak of him as evil but I do not. Evil is following his madness and finding power in it. Evil is a sound mind using Free Will to be like my insane father. Although my father impaled Ethereal with his serpent and ate her soul, an act of insanity, he was not the one who sent her to nothingness. It was Scorpio, wishing to have favor from the hasataan as he consumed her, not my father. I learned of that long after my time in Heaven, and there would come a day where Gloria and I cast Scorpio to nothingness.

When not in his bed, Michael and I cooked meals, gathered fruit and water, visited the Father, and on a very special day he took me to the grotto. Made of crystal the grotto is a place where one goes to contemplate life, the future and the past. It is not like any other place I know of. It is a large dome that is pure crystal and it is alive. It hears your truth and can reflect your experiences, hopes and dreams as you sit within it. That is what we did.

As we walked in I marveled as the crystals were showing reflections of our moments together. Such thoughts were in both of our minds and we watched ourselves making love and saw the way we felt when touched or hearing what the other said. If something Michael said to me made me feel wanted, the image was of him reaching to me and holding me. The images showed both what happened and what we felt at the same time.

Wanting to know all we could of each other the grotto revealed all that was. As we sat, I would ask Michael questions about his existence. The crystals would fall in slivers and make shapes to recreate the places thought of, and they reflected Visions of moments from afar, not from Michael's eyes. I saw when he was first created and walked to meet the Father. I saw him looking at Ethereal when she was created as the next Angel and could see their love for each other. More events and times were shown and I delighted seeing Gloria when little. She was the same when quite small as she was when we met. Then the images of the fall, losing Ethereal, his visit to abaddon on the day my father created it, and how Michael became the Archangel. The more the crystals revealed the more love I had for him. It was as if I had been with him through all his joys and trials.

Once showing us meeting under the apple tree, the crystals flew to their dome and I knew Michael would start asking of my existence.

As he did, the dome changed to be as if we were in abaddon and it was terrifying yet Michael knew we weren't there as it was a reflection. Crystals fell from above and formed a giant serpent that looked as if real. It slithered around us and then formed a stream of crystals that were white shooting through the universe. Each thought, every memory became images and shapes that put us in the places and times we talked of. We watched my father in a place with 100 young girls of Earth, all blonde, all beautiful, all virgins. He had them lined up in two rows as he unleashed his serpent to where it was long past them as they all worshiped it then kissed and licked it. They began climbing onto it and riding it, rubbing themselves to orgasm on it and having 100 likenesses of Gloria worship his serpent made him cum in a spasm that shot his seed through all eternity and landed in the desert of his own mind. In that wet patch of sand, I rose. It was hard for me to see myself when he appeared as I was begging to fuck him and suck his serpent. I knew nothing other and Michael understood that.

Then came reflections of me being *She Who Must Never Be Seen* as I wandered the Earth doing my father's will. He saw the isolation and loneliness I endured as I could show myself to none. Then there was the time when I performed the Ritual with Scorpio, his castration, Gloria appearing to me, then my father making his plan and me going to Heaven and meeting Michael. I had spoke true of the events yet watching them with the crystals forming the events and feelings allowed Michael to understand me in a way I could not do.

Know that I suggested stopping there. What had yet to be shown was the day of the fall and the suffering of Ethereal and seeing my father become the monster he is. That would be too hard to see even for me. As I said that to Micheal the crystals formed as teardrops falling around us. It was what I was feeling inside.

Speaking to Michael I said that Gloria, him, me… we live in the shadow of the fall. Our existence was shaped by what my father had done. I told him that I wanted to be with Gloria and fight alongside of her. At that moment the dome changed to the landscape of all existence and filling the universe was Gloria, her wings larger than galaxies, Blade raised, her expression fierce. As she flapped the crystal Wings all evil blew away. We watched all of the depth of abaddon surrender to her Will and it turned to grains of sand and abaddon was blown away… but then the crystals formed the face of my father and he was sucking the grains of sand from all of abaddon to empower his madness.

Standing up, Michael looked up to the dome and asked it to stop showing all things. We needed no more.

Taking his hand, we walked away and I asked him if all seen had helped him in some way.

"Much I knew. I learned most about you. Your creation, why you are here. Elsa, the grotto can show and reflect our thoughts. It can show the past through our eyes and thinking. What it can't do is show the future. What we worry the future may be."

Understanding all he said, I batted my eyes, and said that there is no way to see the future. We shape the future along with all others. He nodded, sadly, knowing the battle was far from over. I looked at him and tugged at his arm to stop. Pointing to a shady grove of trees we went and sat looking at each other.

"I wish to battle with Gloria. I know my father more than any other. I am small, but my hurt is as large as Gloria's."

Thinking of it, he smiled at me and said just the wanting is how the future is shaped. Then he said he was certain Gloria would find solace fighting together. That made me smile. She had the weight of all sin and evil on her and was alone as she always had been. I told him why only I could fight with her.

"My father has made it clear he will not harm his Sweetness. Only the ones she loves. He will not harm me. He will harm the ones I love or who love me. In that we are true sisters. We are both fighting the same evil."

All I said moved him, and once more we found ourselves in embrace and showing each other love. It was as if Michael knew he may lose me as his passion was more intense than ever. The look in his eyes, the way he held me, holding on to me as if it was our last embrace.

In full Union, I became fully Knowing of what my father had sent me to Heaven for.

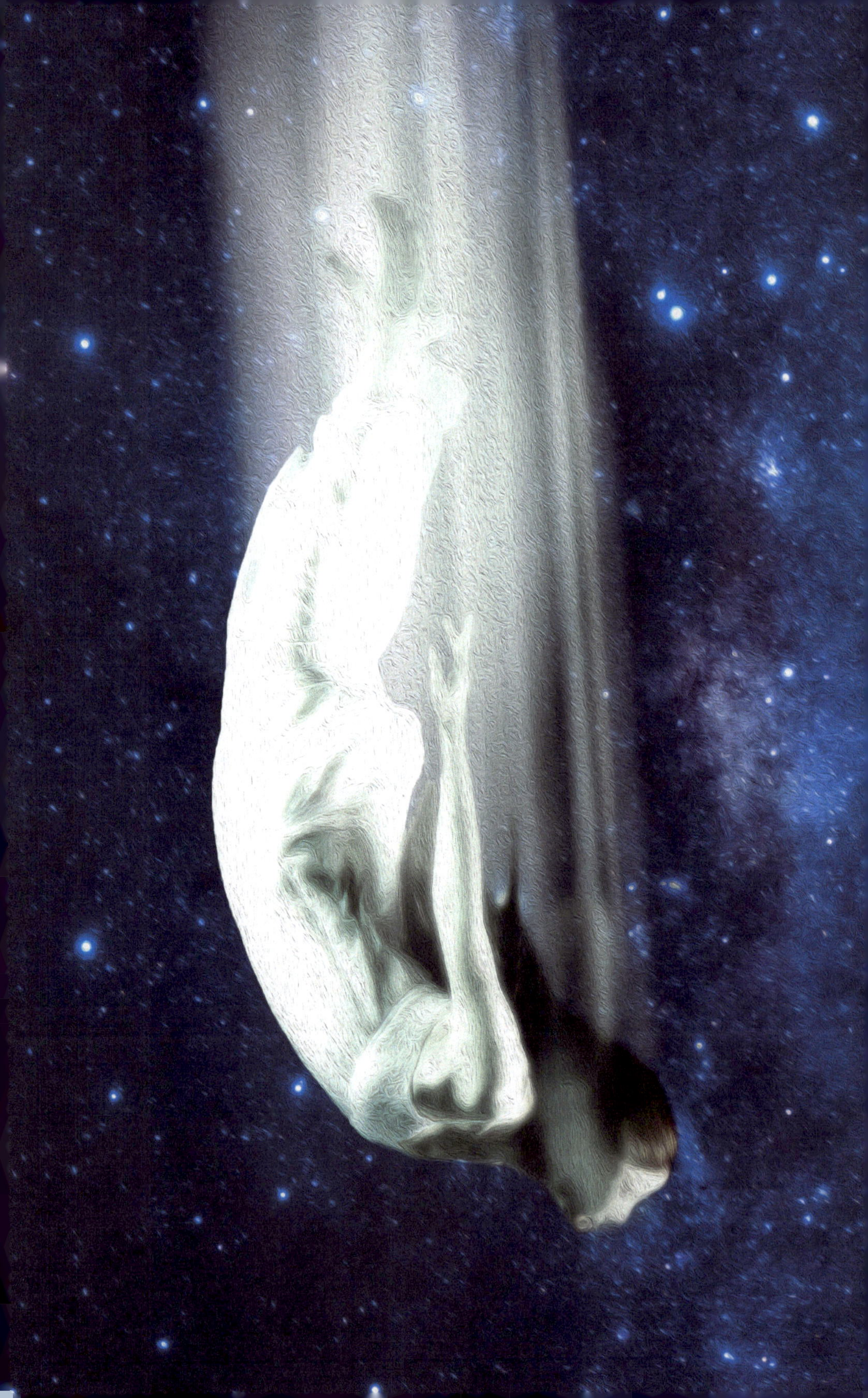

Scroll XVI
Pulling Us

Know I was told to break Michael's heart then run from him. Hurt him. My father knew I would not do that to the one I loved and was destined for. He couldn't take Michael as he was in Heaven where no evil may enter.

As we made love beyond Knowing, Michael in deep as me as two could be in Union, we became One. One heart, one mind, one love.

That is when I became Knowing for I felt the tug at my neck. It was in Union, when we became one, that I felt the pull. Then I knew that when my father pulled me from Heaven and into the madness of his mind, it would not only be me. As one, it would be both me and Michael. He would pull me from Heaven, and he would pull Michael with me.

In that instant I felt the tug, I pulled off of Michael and began running down the path to the waterfall. If I stayed my father would take Michael. If I left, he would not be pulled with me. I had no choice for I loved Michael more than my existence. I cared not what my father did to me but I would not let him have my true love.

Michael took Wing and flew after me, calling out to come back. I did not reply nor did I stop. That is what my father wanted me to do. To surrender to my love of Michael.

To love someone I knew I must make it where Michael believed that I was running from him as I told him I would. Telling him that as one we would both be pulled to my father would have him in danger. It was better to break his heart than stay one more instant. I had no choice. To take care of the one I loved, I ran as he followed above me, begging me to stop. I said not a word. I ran and he was calling that I was safe. No. I wasn't. He wasn't. He didn't understand and if he did… if he touched me… took my hand… any contact my father would pull us to his sick mind.

Reaching the waterfall I was crying and my heart was gone from me. My father hadn't pulled my existence from me for he had pulled my heart and love from me.

Without stopping, I let my beautiful white silk Gloria had graced me with fall from me and be taken by the wind as I jumped from where Heaven stopped and I fell to all eternity without my love and my dreams.

Falling through Eternity I let myself tumble and care not about where I would land. There was no good place for me. I wished only to be as far from Michael as I could be so he would be safe. My hair was loose and it was most often in front of my eyes and I saw nothing of the infinite space between Heaven and abaddon. Between Holy and sin. I was falling. Like Ethereal had fallen to save little Gloria by leaving her behind in Heaven, telling my father she would take Gloria with her and fall with him. I was falling to save Michael. It hurt my being to know that he would lose me as he had lost Ethereal, but like Ethereal I was falling to save the one loved, not break their hearts.

As I fell I caught glimpses of lights when passing through the stars and planets the Father had made in the beginning and they gave me comfort as they had me thinking of how loving He had been to me. I was Knowing what a Father was at last, and why my father was more insane than I could ever understand. To lose such love was madness.

As the lights of the universe faded to nothingness, I heard a sound that stunned me. At the same moment the blackness all around me in the void grew brighter than I have ever known. Then I saw beautiful Wings filling the vastness of nothingness. They circled me, cradling me, holding me. With me, holding the white silk I had cast off as I left Heaven was Gloria. I cannot describe how that felt. In nothingness was light. In despair, I was filled with hope. Seeing her looking at me I felt love of a friend. A sister. One who I would fight with and have no fear.

Looking at me with admiration, she Willed my white silk on me and stopped my descent.

"What you did is as wondrous as my mother did for me. You will not fall to his madness, and you will be loved again. I know all that you did to keep my father safe. I have a true friend and a warrior to join me."

"Gloria, I decided to break your father's heart rather than have him taken by my father. I learned he was doing that and all I could do is save him by falling. How… How did you know?"

Both floating in the warmth and light of her Wings, she looked me in my eyes.

"I flew to abaddon and confronted all the minions there and called for him. With the new Blade, I was there to strike. He rose from the black granite and took form in front of me. He knew my might yet showed no fear. He held up his hand and it was holding the other end of the chain around your neck. He looked at me and said if I struck him, with the chain in his hand I would send not only him to nothingness but also you and my father. I had Vision of you both in embrace and in true Union. All three of you were bound by the chain and then I saw your face as you felt the tug… knew what he was doing… then watched you run. I have never seen such love before. I saw your face and it is the saddest thing I have ever seen… sadder than when I learned of Ethereal. I know what it is to lose someone you love. I speak true. If I could have saved my mother by doing what you did, I would have. You were doing what I would do now."

Know that I cried as never before. She understood. She loved me.

She wanted to be like me. I wanted to be like her. I wiped my eyes with the white silk, and she smiled saying she knew it would be most useful one day. That had me laughing with her.

"Gloria, we are bound. We fight the same fight. Before he devises a new evil, let us find him and stop him forever."

Scroll XVII
The Hurt

Know we searched for what humans would consider a thousand years but never found my father. At first I was certain he had escaped into his mind, his own abaddon. I was free to enter there, and I did many times but never found him. Using his most effective guises he was being the great deceiver. Gloria and I both knew that he was nothing more than a coward. He could harm all who existed yet never wished to be bold, stand and fight, take anyone with power. He fed on the weak.

There came a time when we both knew he was not in abaddon or his own mind. He was hiding in the open, causing no harm as the harm he started with sin lived on without him. The humans glorified his ways and that made it hard to see if any were him.

Time has no meaning to Angels or ones gone from Earth. All that exists are a series of events. Moments, words, feelings, and they may be connected or only isolated incidents. Gloria Willed us to a rock on the edge of nothing where eternity ended and the nothingness that was before the Father thought of something. We cast our gaze down to the universe below and looked for the one unique light that was the fire within my father but we could not see him in all creation.

"He's not gone, Gloria. He's taken a new form. He was once a beautiful First Angel, then became the hasataan, then the deceiver. He's waiting."

Nodding, Gloria thought of what I had said and agreed with it. She closed her eyes and waited for a Vision of Lucifer. Arranging my white silk, I waited for Gloria's response. Watching Gloria, I continued to understand how badly she was hurt. My father, doing what he was, hurt her more by playing such a game. Watching Gloria's eyes open, I saw she had an idea.

"Elsa, I think the same as you. All we can do is tempt him to reveal himself. I was thinking of what would be most tempting to him."

"You."

Nodding, Gloria looked certain of that.

"Until he reveals himself you will have that chain around your neck. You know what that means."

Gloria's eyes were not sad for me. Time meant nothing to us and I was sure he would appear when he felt he could take Gloria. We both knew until he was destroyed the chain would remain on my throat and I could not be with Michael until it was gone.

"No matter how long it takes I will never put your father in his grasp. Gloria, I will return to my abaddon. The one where I was made. Only there will Michael be safe from me and this chain. My father will be cautious if we are together. He will find you and you will strike him down. On that day come to me and we will return to Heaven. On that day I will be in Union with Michael."

Coming to me, holding me with tenderness she said that she would do no else until she struck my father to nothingness. She asked to see my abaddon, and she would rescue me from it on that day. I looked up at her and was filled with love for her. I wished to tell her what I have longed to say since we met. It was a truth that I had only learned after meeting her.

"Gloria, before we go to where I was made I have a truth to tell. I had worried it would cause you sorrow but now I think it may be Joy. Let's sit and I will speak true."

Not questioning me or worried, we went to rocks that we had sat on when talking. She was beautiful and I had watched her change from a girl to a woman. That caused Joy in me and I understood it was more than appreciation of knowing her and watching her become the most beautiful of all in Creation. I smiled at her and told her what I had come to know.

"I have long wondered why you found me and rescued me when you gave me this silk. I also wondered why Michael and the Father had no doubts about me. They accepted me as an Angel. That was a surprise yet I thought it only that they were loving and kind and blamed me not for being made by Lucifer. Gloria, when you first looked at me, or when you look at me this moment, what do you see?"

Her eyes lit bright and she smiled at me.

"I see wonder. Beauty. I see one as Holy as me. An Angel."

"Yet I am from the one who defiled all that was Holy. He made me to be temptation… but Gloria, not to sad humans… to you… and to Michael. I know now that is what he did, and I know why I was loved without caution by the Father, Michael, and you. It is what he made me from…"

Sitting, looking confused and uncertain of my meaning, I thought it best to continue and let her know without stopping.

"He wanted me as a way to you. When he made me he knew that I must be welcomed in Heaven and those who love me now. I will speak of the saddest moment I know. The day of the fall he ate your mother's soul. All she was… all her goodness and her Glory became part of him yet he did not use it. He kept it hidden. When he made me, I was made with the soul of Ethereal. She is in me. She is me. We are one. That is why Michael could love me without feeling he betrayed Ethereal. He didn't. She is here in me and why I am Angel, not demon. I am not the same as her and I have my own soul but I feel her always in the way I show love. The way I feel about you. The way I love Michael. I am sure Father knows she is in me. Ethereal is not gone. Gloria, she lives on in me."

Know I have never seen such tears of love and Joy as the ones Gloria cried as I spoke true.

"Elsa… All this time I wondered why you were a mystery. From a place so bad yet you are the most caring and loving one I have known since… well, it has been answered… since my mother left me. You are lit by her spirit and have her love. Do you think Michael knows?"

All I could do is shake my head.

"The Father has not told him, nor have I. Gloria, I think it best that way. I am not Ethereal. I don't want him to love me because her spirit is part of me. It is a Blessing and I felt it right to tell you. Gloria, imagine being me and loved because Michael thinks me Ethereal? I would be nothing. I am not nothing. That was what my father wanted me to be. I am Elsa. There will be a time I will speak true I feel her inside of me, and why. I want only to be loved as who I am. I see the spirit of Ethereal in you for you are her daughter and from her. I speak true, we are sisters. We both have her in us."

After many tears and holding each other, we smiled for we understood that we were bound to each other and would be Knowing why. We stood, and I Willed us to my abaddon. It was sand and nothing more. No longer the grains of my father's mind. It was just a desert where I would stay until my father was no more. I knelt in the sand and as the wind blew, Gloria's wings grew large and filled the sky. She flapped them with such force as to blow all the grains away. I marveled at what she had done. Without the madness of my father there, and without the grains of sand, I was in a place that was green with grasses and plants. It was an oasis in the desert that I never knew was there. I looked at Gloria with wonder.

"Elsa, you were in the desert in Egypt for a time long. You know that in a desert there must be an oasis. You really need to be gifted with your own Wings!"

Coming to me, we hugged, and she told me to reach in the pocket of my white silk sheath. I wondered what she meant but did as she asked. In the pocket was the brown parchment and string she had given to me the day we met. It contained something once again. I looked up at her, then down at the package and unwrapped it.

Inside was a picture of Michael, Ethereal and little Gloria. I looked at it and cried for it was a gift greater than any. It was a picture of me as well.

Raising her right hand up to the now blue sky above me, her Wings gently lifted her, one leg slightly up, and I watched her loving smile as she ascended to eternity to find and strike down my father.

Know that I wait for that day and Know she shall put an end to my suffering, and hers.